Y Signal

JD Cowan

For the New Lost Generation (1979-1989)

TABLE OF CONTENTS

Y Signal

Why Not

It's just another day, but not for you. The other kids are out playing, and their excited shouts fill the stuffed schoolyard. Recess always brings out the best in everyone. You laze under the boughs of your favorite tree with hands nestled behind your head and just listen. Singing birds and roaring car motors remind you that the neighborhood is alive.

One of your friends might be calling your name somewhere out there in the chaos, but it doesn't matter right now. You're here, and everything's fine. There's always the next recess.

The soft, freshly watered grass under your shorts and scuffed-up red sneakers make you comfortable. You cross your legs, close your eyes, and take the oncoming summer in.

You can smell the humidity building—only weeks until school lets out. But it won't be out forever. You're not that lucky. Your eyebrow twitches at that realization. It's okay, though. Autumn is a ways away. Why bother worrying now?

A soft breeze carrying the scent of a nearby barbecue grill makes your mouth water just a bit. Porterhouse steak. You just had lunch, but it was only a lousy bologna sandwich. Maybe Mom will cook some steak tonight. Heck, maybe Dad will decide to order pizza! The sky is the limit.

Bells ring from the nearby church. They seem to rattle with the constant beat in the back of your brain. It's about time to pick up a new CD or two—the old ones are getting samey. One of the guys mentioned a catchy song playing on the radio recently. What was it called, again? Oh well, one more mowed lawn, and you'll have enough to get whatever it is you need. Heck, there should be enough extra to spend at the arcade. They might have gotten some new games recently.

Today is Friday, and tonight there's a familiar television block waiting for you at home. You also have your pick of cartoons on Saturday morning. The weekend schedule is packed with much to do. Time to kick back and relax. Everything is lining up just right.

In the corners of your mind, a tinge tickles your thoughts. You're supposed to be remembering something important, but it remains just out of reach. Is it homework? Did Mom ask you to do the dishes? Maybe, maybe not. It could be anything. You brush the thought away. You can deal with that later. Why bother worrying now?

The school bell rings, and the sounds of children silence as they slip away like water down the drain. They're gone now, and you're alone. No big deal, they'll be back. They always come back, and they always will.

But there you remain, sitting under your favorite tree. You could get up, but there's no need. They won't notice one kid sitting alone outside.

You open your eyes to catch fat puffs of white clouds drifting through the harsh beams of sunlight in the bright blue sky. The summer heat makes you sigh. That sun is merciless today. You might as well be sitting in a desert.

However, none of that is important at this moment. Why worry about any of it? The weekend is near.

The silence overtakes your busy thoughts as you slip into slumber.

You could wake up.
But why bother?

Y Signal

Part One
One Future

"It wasn't as good as I expected it to be."

Ray didn't disagree with his friend's assessment. Ever since they were little kids, the group of boys had enjoyed going to the movies during their summer vacation. It was a break from the snore-fest that was school. They were free from prison! Paradise had arrived.

This summer of 1995, however, had felt somewhat *off*. Ray couldn't put his finger on why. This movie continued that oddly detached feeling that had clung to him. Why wasn't it the way it was supposed to be?

Batman Forever was fine, he supposed, but there was a piece missing from the picture. He'd still rent it when Ultratech Video II got it on the shelves in a few months, certainly. It just . . . wasn't that good. Of course, it wouldn't ruin his fifth-grade summer vacation, nothing could, but he expected better. Summer was supposed to be perfect. That was just the way it was and always had to be. There was no sense wasting time thinking about things—that was for school. And school was over. He just couldn't shake the impression that something wasn't quite right.

Ray scratched his towheaded mushroom hair and looked towards the western sun setting over the smattering of suburban houses dotted with well-manicured maple trees. The warmer temperatures of summer always comforted him, as did the familiar sights of his hometown. Tomorrow was Saturday, not that it made a difference during vacation, and he would be visiting his grandmother. Things were as normal as they always were. If there was a problem, then it had to be in his own dumb head.

"Ray!" Danny called from down on the road. Their blonde-haired friend looked up at him as he tied his red sneakers. The scab on his knee looked to be healing well. He got that one from climbing fences over by the mall a few days ago. "Where are you going, Ray? I thought we were hitting the arcade before the teenagers got there. *Mortal Kombat II*, remember?"

Ray looked at his three friends and thought for a moment. There was already a mistake here. "How come you didn't say *Mortal Kombat 3* instead? It just came out, right?"

"Are you kidding?" George said. Ray's shorter friend pushed up the scuffed glasses on his nose and sighed. His freckles and wild hair always made him look like he had just fallen into a dirt pile. "You know why, Ray. MK3 blows. The new characters and stages are so lame. It doesn't do anything new. Midway barely even tried. They didn't even put in Scorpion!"

Danny laughed. "Yeah, and Stryker looks like my dad."

"No new girls on the level of Mileena or Kitana, either," Andrew mused. The tallest boy laughed as he looked upon his three friends. "No idea what they were thinking with that one. The editor in that one letter column in ProGamer Monthly called us ingrates for complaining. Feels weird that they didn't get it. I thought everyone got how much of a letdown that one was."

"That's just it, guys!" Ray said. He couldn't figure out why exasperation nipped at him so hard, but he knew he was close to figuring it out. "Something's been off this year, don't you think? Usually, things get better, right? Super Nintendo, *Terminator 2*, *Sonic the Hedgehog 3*, the next season of *The Simpsons* . . . my Dad always tells me that's how it always was when he was growing up. We're always getting better, and things always improve. He's gotta be right. Burroughsvale is a much better place than when he was a kid. But the stuff we've been getting recently is kinda . . . lame, right? It's 1995, but it doesn't feel like much has changed from last year."

Danny and George both sighed and waved him off.

"You're always so paranoid," George said. "Spend some more time in nature and you'll realize how silly a lot of this is."

Danny rolled his eyes. "There goes the boy scout again. Listen, Ray, you just gotta toughen up like me and Andrew here." He pretended to throw a few punches. The shorter boy in the tank-top shuffled about as if he were a boxer. "You can fight anything with enough training."

"Uh huh, sure," Andrew said. He laughed. "You play too many video games, Danny."

"No such thing! If we all took a boxing or karate class we would be the toughest kids in school. Almost as tough as Andrew here."

Andrew winced. "Shut up, man. Don't bring that garbage up now. It's summer."

Both Danny and George continued excitedly talking about the movie that they clearly liked more than Ray did as they turned back down Maple Street. Perhaps he really was imagining this whole issue. Why spoil a good time for the others? He decided to just drop the subject. The evening was here, and it was time to relax.

"Oh shoot," George said. He scratched at the long hair under his baseball cap. "Forgot I'm supposed to head straight back home. Mom wants me to pack for the camping trip next week. They really seem to like going cross-country. Anybody want to stay over tonight? I can convince her if it's only one of you mooks."

Ray dismissed the thought as soon as he considered it. "I've got someone to meet right now."

"Of course you do. You city slickers are always busy."

Andrew laughed. "Just because you like nature doesn't make you a country boy, George. Just like how liking playing beat 'em up games doesn't make Danny a tough guy. Are you ever taking those boxing classes you keep going on about, Dan?"

"I'll get to it!" Danny said. "It's summer, right? This time of the year is for kicking back, not getting pumped up."

George cleared his throat. "Hello? I asked a question, morons."

"I guess I'm up for it." Danny sighed and rolled his eyes. He scratched at the scab on his elbow. "You've still got *Turtles in Time* rented, right? I never get sick of that one."

Andrew laughed at his two friends. "Go ahead, Danny. I'm going to pass. The movie kinda wore me out. Be sure to catch a bear for me, George. I've got just a place on the wall for it, and it's sure to impress the ladies."

"My mom would kill me." George chuckled. He waved to his friends and took off in the opposite direction. Danny sprinted after his faster friend. "See you guys in a week or so."

Their two friends disappeared into the maze of suburban homes across the street from the sidewalk. Ray watched them go, thinking about what George had said. Camping was fun, but they did it all the time in the Scouts, didn't they? They could go any time, but why now during peak summer? The kid would be missing all the good times. Parents just didn't get it: Friday nights, summer nights, were for fun. Everyone knew this down to their bones.

"Hey, Ray!" Andrew softly punched Ray on the shoulder. "You're going to meet your cousin, aren't ya? Mind if I come with? My 'rents aren't going to be home for another hour or two. They're still at that retreat."

Ray reflexively rubbed his shoulder. It didn't hurt, but his friend never really hit him that hard to begin with. Andrew was taller than him and tended to scare a lot of kids at school, especially when he wore his sleeveless shirts that showed some of the cuts on his arms he had gotten in playground fights. Ray knew better. Andrew tended to be quiet and intimidating when he wasn't with his friends, but he paid attention to what was going on. He wouldn't want to go anywhere unless he had an ulterior motive. Perhaps he thought the movie being bad was weird, too. As silly as it was, a summer movie being bad was just not supposed to be.

"What about your babysitter?" Ray asked.

"It's not Kim Bergeron, so I don't care. *This* girl's a skag. Total melon head. She's always whining about not having a boyfriend, too. Not that it matters, I don't need a babysitter. I'm going to be a sixth grader in a few months. Parents don't get it."

"Barney likes her."

"Golden retrievers like anyone. That's why they're so dumb."

"Alright, you can come," Ray said. The overhanging streetlights popped on around them. He ignored how strange of a sight that was in the bright sun of the summer evening. It wasn't even close to being dark yet! "Just remember that my cousin doesn't like being stared at, alright? Lenny is a weird guy."

"After seeing Jim Carrey in that weird movie, I think I'm prepared for anything."

The two boys descended the near-empty street down the sidewalk, just as the sky turned orange. Ray would never get over how different summer was from winter. Where then it would be pitch dark by the time his parents turned on the six o'clock news: now it took until near nine for the sun to finally disappear, long after the little kids already went to bed. It was like the world wanted him to stay out longer. Of course, Ray wouldn't argue with a big world much older and wiser than he! It was just bad luck that his parents always turned him down when he wanted to be out later. They watched too much television: no one had ever been kidnapped in Burroughsvale. It was just another mid-sized town like any other in the boring '90s, in the boring modern world. Dullsville! Even as the two kids moved down the sidewalk, they saw plenty of other kids and teenagers moving to and fro down neighboring streets wearing their casual summer clothes. Nothing would ever happen here, and he really was thankful for that. Summers were made for boring towns like this. That is one thing that would never change.

Down the sloping hill, they passed the convenience store the Conte family owned. Two summers ago, Ray's friends bought far too many sugary snack treats and, after a game of war in the grass field behind Mary Gardner Elementary, the lot of kids indulged in said victory spoils. Ray couldn't even look at food again for near a month afterwards, and George ended up throwing up all over his aunt's Chihuahua later that night. Both Andrew and Danny received killer headaches that begat heavy questioning from their parents. Crazy times. The four still went out for cokes every now and then, but never again did they do something that stupid. Ray figured this was what his parents called growing up. He sure didn't feel any smarter, though.

"Lenny?" Andrew suddenly asked. "Isn't he the one that was a roadie for some cool bands and found that awesome stuff you used to bring to school presentations?"

"He's my dad's oldest brother's kid, and he just moved here a couple of weeks ago. Weird guy, but he used to find some neat stuff to share with me when he was out on the road. He gave me that Gin Blossoms record before they hit it big. Dude's always been my favorite cousin."

Many times Ray thought on the time he had pneumonia in first grade, and laid in bed alone for that week, it was Lenny who stayed to keep him company. They listened to some of Lenny's records he got from the bands he toured with, and the boy learned about rock music for the first time. They also played a lot of Jackal on the NES. Ever since then, Ray had a soft spot for his older cousin.

Andrew hummed an old song to himself. "If I remember, he also said the lead singer of the Gin Blossoms would kill himself, and then the poor guy did right before the guys at school even heard of that album. That cousin of yours is strange but interesting."

"It was the guitarist, not the singer, and it was just a guess from what a friend told him. Lenny just has good sixth sense. He probably gets tips from all the people he knows in the industry, though. Anyway, he just called me up a few hours ago to meet him, and we haven't talked since he moved here. He hasn't really talked to anyone. I really wanna know what he found this time, and why he's been so distant."

"I hope he's got an early copy of the next Oasis album. There hasn't been much good radio this year. The last Pearl Jam was just a dud, and U2's taking too long after whatever that one from a few years ago was supposed to be. Hey, maybe you were right about something feeling off recently."

Ray laughed his friend off. "Not now, man. I don't want to think about it."

"Right! It's summer!"

Ray and Andrew hit St. Joseph Street at the bottom of the awkward hill, one of the handier streets in Burroughsvale. It could be considered a main road, since it led towards the main shopping sector and the mall a few blocks over to the east. Eventually it connected through a park and some apartment complexes, as well as going through towards St. Willibrord Elementary, and one of the high schools even further down. It felt like a lot, but it was all he knew. It wasn't a busy street despite being such a vital pathway, but it sure was a handy one. All that fun stuff was to the right of them, but they turned left instead. There they found the mini-mall nestled in suburbia that Ray knew like the back of his hand.

This was the real treasure trove of Burroughsvale that no one ever spoke of, but everyone knew about. Beside the gas station, Ultratech Video (the original one!), the Village of Heroes comic book store, and Sophie's Pizzeria, awaited him like they always would. There was also a dry cleaner squeezed in there, but nobody cared about that. This was the place to be on a Friday night, and it wasn't even on the main strip! It was like a special secret only the cool kids knew about, even though the reality was clearly much different.

"Do you think George will see Sasquatch on his camping trip?" Andrew asked. He always seemed to posit questions out of the blue like this. "The dude loves camping, but he really doesn't like thinking about the cool things hidden out there."

"It's not always about fairies, Andrew. George just likes quiet. Though, to be fair, it's probably more magical out there than here. Burroughsvale is the most boring place on Earth."

Andrew shrugged. "At least Danny should be happy. They've got *Streets of Rage 2* in at Ultratech. That kid over there just brought it in."

The pair passed the video store, which was as packed as ever. Arthur, Shane, and Nick, were in there, probably crowding the Sega Genesis games. Ray saw them in there all the time during the summer. They played those Madden games a lot, but every now and then, they'd talk about an obscure one they'd stumbled into out of town or wherever they went on vacation. *Granada* sounded like a good game, lots of shooting and action, but Ray never had a Sega Genesis—that was Danny's domain. Ray had a Super Nintendo, which sometimes caused arguments. The screaming matches on the playground could be something else among the different camps. Sega or Nintendo: whose side were you on? It didn't matter, though. Video games were just video games. No point in taking them so seriously. In the end, they all got great games, and that's what mattered.

Ray considered going into the Ultratech and checking for a copy of *Donkey Kong Country* to rent, but he wouldn't have the time to play this weekend. Besides, it was always out. Hopefully, that would change when the sequel released. It usually did. Instead, he breezed by the buzzing store towards Sophie's Pizzeria, two shops over.

"Out of the way, boys," a burly adult said.

The middle-aged man had a stack of pizza boxes juggled in his thick arms. He braced them on the roof of his small, black Volkswagen before finally jiggling his keys loose from his pocket. This wasn't that uncommon around here. He must have been late coming home from work and picked this up for his family. Ray's dad was never late, so he couldn't relate to it, but he had seen this sight many times before. This town had all sorts of types.

Before Ray went into the pizzeria, he spotted another man smoking a cigarette by the front door. This thin man was leaning against the wall with his hands cupped behind his head. His dread-locked, long brown hair, black shirt, and torn jean shorts, and pale skin, made him look like some kind of punk, but he only muttered to himself as passersby crept around him. This dude didn't look like he was from around here.

"*99.9. After midnight,*" the weirdo whispered like it was a chant. "*99.9. Listen through the static. 99.9. Listen closely and you'll hear the Y Signal. Damnit, Lenny. What does that mean? Tell me.*"

He repeated himself over and over. Before Ray could say anything about him to Andrew, the thin man saw the boy staring and took off in the opposite direction of the parking to the west. Perhaps, he just needed some change for the bus. But wait, did he say Lenny's name?

"Come on, Ray," Andrew said. He elbowed his friend. "Your cousin's sitting by the back."

Inside, a crowd awaited. A line up at the counter of a few teenagers and some couples patiently waited their turn to order. The delivery guys appeared to be out as Ray overheard several of the employees in the kitchen talking about having no spare cars. There were only about six tables in this narrow shop with checkerboard décor that was about forty years out of date, with framed photos of old rock n' roll guys like Elvis, Gene Vincent, and Buddy Holly, on the walls. but that was the way these places always were and always would be. Despite the packed house, the last table in the back right corner was the only one that had a single person sitting at it. Everyone else was taking their food out.

The young man at the back sat alone. Ray's favorite cousin muttered to himself. "*I told him not to bother, but he just won't listen . . .*"

Ray and Andrew sat across from Lenny, who didn't move at their approach. The creaking wooden chairs cried out as they shifted themselves into place, but still Ray's cousin didn't appear to see them. The two boys dodged the lone waitress on the floor as she made a beeline towards the packed counter. For such a noisy place, Lenny sure was being oblivious.

"Sorry, we're a bit late, man," Ray said. "We were just talking about the movie."

Ray's cousin kept staring at the checkered pattern of the table surface as if he expected it to melt under his weight. "Wasn't very good, huh?"

"Did you see it?" Ray asked.

"No."

That was when Ray noticed his cousin looked off. His blue eyes were bloodshot; his patchy facial hair was unkempt on his square chin, and his light brown hair hadn't been combed. His old Def Leppard shirt had stains all over. Odd red gashes on his white skin made him look as if he hadn't cleaned himself recently.

Lenny rubbed his eyes and yawned. "That *Judge Dredd* movie you're planning to see next week? Don't bother. It's a turkey."

"No way!" Andrew said. He leaned forward on the table. "It has Sly in it, and it's Judge freaking Dredd. It's not that different from *Cobra*, which he was great in! You can't screw up that sure a thing."

Ray didn't want to bring up that they had just seen a Batman movie that wasn't quite as good as they hoped, but he secretly didn't like the one before it either. Maybe Ray was thinking too hard about this. But messing up Judge Dredd, of all things? That was a bit hard to believe. The older kids in the comic shop next door were always raving about the series, going on about the cool future setting and hardcore action. How could the movie men get that wrong, and with Sylvester Stallone, of all people! It didn't make sense.

"Come on, are you serious?" Ray asked. "Did you see some early reviews? Maybe you talked to someone who saw it early?"

Lenny shook his head. "No. I just know the future. It's all thanks to the Y Signal."

By the time Ray realized what his cousin had just said, the waitress returned with two slices of pepperoni pizza and placed it in front of the disheveled man. Andrew sat with his arms folded glaring at Ray from the corner of his eye. He was signaling that he wanted to leave, but there was no sense in doing that. Lenny didn't lie.

But he also never looked this bad.

Ray's favorite cousin now wore scuffed blue jeans and old sneakers. The old watch their grandfather had given him that he usually wore was missing. His nose was bright red, as were his normally blue eyes, on his flushed face.

"I know I sound crazy," he said to the two children. Lenny took a bite of pizza and wretched. Sophie's was always good, which made his over-the-top reaction strange. However, his distaste didn't stop him from chewing on the slice while speaking. "I have to tell someone before it happens. So let's start here. Yarbrough, the guitarist for the Panorama Agents, left me his old radio when he vanished back in 1992, and I've been using it recently. That's when it started."

13

Andrew's mouth fell open. "The guy who disappeared after the band hit it big three years ago? Wrote all those dark songs that even Kurt Cobain complained about? No one's seen him in years, and even the band moved on without him. Their last album came out last year, and it was full of songs he wrote before he vanished. Come to think of it, wasn't that album called *Y Signal*?"

"I know, junior. I was a roadie for them the year before he disappeared. I was just a dumb twenty-year-old who had plenty of experience on the road. It feels like another life—a life before the Y Signal."

"Y Signal?" Andrew asked. "What is that? No one ever got why they called the album that."

Lenny groaned. "Never mind. Forget I said anything."

"Everyone thought Yarbrough committed suicide," Ray said. He scrunched his nose. Ray hated that he remembered such morbid things. "But he took all his money out of his bank accounts before he disappeared, so I don't really buy it. Still, that radio has to be worth something."

"Not really, Ray. You can probably get it used at Radio Shack for a couple of bucks today. It was made in '89, and the tape deck is busted. Only the radio works. There's nothing unique about the piece of junk."

Ray sighed. This was going nowhere. "So then why are you telling us all this?"

"I'm telling you because I'm working on something that is about to blow up in a big way. Wheels are rolling. Don't worry if you don't see me in a few days, is what I'm saying."

"Does it have anything to do with the guy that was outside? He was muttering your name."

Lenny's eyes widened, and his mouth tightened. He cleared his throat before taking another bite of his slice. "Did you talk to him?"

"No, who is he?"

"Long story. Just keep away from him. You've probably heard that weirdos from out of town keep showing up in Burroughsvale. They're all like him. Be sure to avoid them." He pushed aside his empty plate. "Anyways, I'm telling you this in case you don't see me again. I might get called out of town suddenly. Tell your dad not to worry if I disappear. If you don't see me for a few days, check in with Billy. I've got him in my address book back at my apartment. He's been waiting for the update. Let him know that we found it."

Ray cocked his eyebrow. "None of this makes any sense."

"None of it does, yeah." Lenny shrugged. "Get used to it."

"Get used to what?" Andrew asked.

Lenny paused. "Life is a dream, desperate to be swept away. Dew-covered grass in the morning is always withered by night. But we ain't grass!"

"No, we're not grass," Ray said. He tried to process the insanity of that statement as best as he could. "We're much more than that."

"Exactly." Lenny grinned. "And I'm going to prove it."

Before any further questions could be asked, Ray's cousin shot out of his chair, put some money on the counter, and bolted out of the pizzeria. Both Ray and Andrew were left looking after him with far more questions than answers. It wasn't like Lenny hadn't been flaky before, but Ray couldn't help but have a bad feeling in his stomach about this one. Perhaps his cousin just missed life out on the road. Ray let the thought slip from his mind. It wasn't his business. Lenny was just being weird. The two boys left the pizzeria.

The pair shared chatter on the way home, but their minds were clearly elsewhere. They kept to themselves as they passed along the bike path and the park, slipping through public designated walkways back home. The sun had almost left the sky, and Ray's parents always wanted him home before dark. They just watched too much *Unsolved Mysteries*. Nothing would happen to anyone in Burroughsvale, and that's the way he liked it.

Andrew separated from Ray, disappearing down Gerald Way, into the outstretched giant oaks that covered the street. He could hear Barney barking excitedly close by. Some older kids were still playing street hockey, as they tended to do most days during the summer. Ray continued on to St. Hubert just a few streets away.

When he got home, both his parents chided him for being a bit late. His younger brother was already sleeping, as four-year-old kids tend to do at this time. Ray told his dad about his meeting, but this father didn't pay his son much mind.

"Lenny has always been eccentric," he said. "Let him figure out his own problems. It's past eight, Ray. Head on up to your room.

No staying up late. Remember that you're going to visit your grandma tomorrow."

"I know, Dad."

But Ray couldn't relax. The more he thought about Lenny, the more he felt awkward about what happened. He went to bed at 9pm but ended up sitting up for an hour staring out his window onto the summer street below. His parents departed to their room around an hour later, leaving the house quiet and creaking in the night. Still, he couldn't quite settle down.

The lamppost light cast hard white beams on the empty road. The sight reminded him of a certain album cover Lenny had lent him once. The Panorama Agents. Ray remembered those harsh abrasive sounds with unbelievably angry lyrics that sounded like how Ray imagined everyone in high school talked like. Aggressive music for hopeless people who hated the very idea of the future. They all just sounded so depressed. Didn't they know how great the future was going to be?

That was what the older kids liked, though. Ray preferred sunnier music; he still got chided for listening to old bands like Icon, Def Leppard, or Boston, but he understood why younger groups like the Panorama Agents were popular. What he didn't get was why Yarbrough's disappearance bothered him more than it did for actual fans of the band.

At school, Andrew, Paul, and Wayne, really went on about how they liked the Panorama Agents, though they said the most recent album they put out last year sounded odd without Yarbrough. The band used lyrics and songs he left behind, but the album title was weird. For some reason, they called it *Y Signal*, based on a phrase Yarbrough used a lot, in the months before he disappeared. In many ways, it sounded like the poor guy was still around, even though no one had seen him since 1992.

"It's midnight . . ." Ray said to no one. The clock ticked aggressively above his bed. Time always moved, whether he noticed it or not. "Already."

He couldn't help but be curious. What was his cousin saying talking about a Y Signal? That guy outside the pizzeria was muttering to himself about Lenny and numbers, too. Those numbers sounded like prices . . . or a radio station. Is that what Lenny was listening to? Did that have something to do with the radio Yarbrough left to Ray's cousin? The boy needed to clear this up, or else he would never get to sleep. Was Lenny actually in trouble? This had to be some kind of misunderstanding. Ray's dad always said this he got carried away by kid stuff.

What was it the punk said? Ray thought back. "*99.9. After midnight. 99.9. Listen through the static. 99.9. Listen closely and you'll hear the Y Signal.*"

99.9? Was he really talking about a radio station? Yeah, right. Sure, he was. Ray laughed it off. That guy was just paranoid.

Ray didn't believe it, but he couldn't stop thinking about the possibility. He should just go to bed. But just in case . . .

It was difficult to see so late, especially since he didn't want to wake his parents, so Ray slipped out of bed while keeping certain to step lightly around his room. The summer warmth made the place feel like a heat box, but thankfully his Bart Simpson boxers and undershirt were enough to keep the humid weather at bay. They didn't have air conditioning or much in the way of fans, which made sliding around his room more frustrating than he preferred, especially when he forgot to put away his things. Nonetheless, he soon adjusted to his surroundings.

Ray stepped around his left-out Nintendo controllers and his old notepad of game notes, narrowly missing landing on that tape of *No Retreat No Surrender 2* that Lenny had found on his trip to New York five years ago. That was a great flick. Even his friends dug that one. It reminded Ray why he had to do this. Lenny had done so much for him, so it was only right that he return the favor.

The old radio waited in the corner of his room beside the twelve-inch TV. He sat before it and folded his legs in the usual position. A deep breath escaped him as he let the insanity of this situation sink in. No one could possibly be as dumb as he was at this very moment. Ray plugged in his Walkman headphones and turned the station to 99.9.

A burst of static caused him to flinch. He had half-expected an exhausted radio DJ ranting about parties he was missing by staying up so late. Yet, there was nothing. Apparently, radio stations went off the air at a certain hour. Not that he knew anything about how adults worked. Eventually, the fuzz smoothed out, and he sat still on his bedroom floor just listening to the world of noise before him. Was he doing something wrong?

Sparks flashed in his brain as the din rose and fell with his breathing. Nothing but an endless fuzz in a cacophonous dissonance festival that kicked about before him. He concentrated, but nothing broke through the wall.

"What a waste of time."

Perhaps his cousin was just pulling his leg. It wouldn't be the first time. Lenny did like to play pranks, like the time at his grandmother's birthday party when the jerk kept putting whoopee cushions on Ray's seat. That hadn't happened since Ray was seven, but people don't change. At least, that's what his dad told him.

Ray yawned, his mind spinning with fatigue. That punk at the pizzeria was just some kind of head case. Enough of this—it was time for bed.

Then, just as he sat up, he thought he heard a whisper. Ray cocked his ear and listened close as a voice spoke deep in the pit. Slowly, it rose in volume. Ray recognized the source. He sat still and concentrated.

The boy focused his mind on the small speck of clarity in the tidal wave of fuzz. It swirled around him like a tornado of incomprehensibility. Eventually, the noise parted like the Red Sea, leaving him with nothing but low whispers to fill the gaps of overbearing silence. The longer he listened the more it cleared up.

"*—and do you think anyone can help you?*" the voice said. "*The future is coming, regardless of how much you shut your eyes to the truth! Planes boring into buildings, secret assassinations of pivotal politicians, and even your entertainment turning against you . . . whatever you can imagine is a possibility in the madness to come.*"

Ray listened close, but the raving lunacy of what the voice was saying remained impenetrable to a fifth grader. It wasn't unlike the political debates he sometimes heard his dad listening to on his own radio. Ray could hear the words crystal clear, but all he heard was nonsense.

"*Yugoslavia will be blown to bits. Towers will explode over your modern Meccas. Your school might very well be shot to pieces. And that's just some of what is coming soon. What can you do against it? Nothing. But you can save yourself from this fate. This is why you are listening to the broadcast right now. Welcome to the Y Signal, ladies and gentlemen, where you will learn the path towards a future free of strife and hardship. I have found the path, and so will you.*

This world doesn't deserve you. But I know one that does."

The last words hit Ray like a freight train. He knew who this was! It was the very man everyone had thought disappeared years ago—the man who dropped off the planet. Ray was listening to the old guitarist and lyricist of the Panorama Agents, Yarbrough. He was actually alive.

And he was insane.

"The End is on the way, everyone," Yarbrough said. *"Be vigilant. This will only hurt the first time, but once you leave it all behind, it will feel so much better."*

A squeal of static pierced Ray's brain, and he clasped his ears against his brain. He tried to throw the headphones off, but it was too late. A tsunami of red pain crashed into his eyes, nose, and mouth, and slipped into his brain. Ray thought he might have cried out, but there was no way to know. An invisible force had attacked him.

When he slumped over, the music was already playing in his mind: "Motorcycle Future" from the 1988 self-titled album of the Panorama Agents. Squealing guitars and a ferocious beat tumbled into his mind like the apocalypse running a marathon. The only thing he could remember was how much he hated that song before his senses left him behind for the darkness. The world was being taken for a ride into the deep night of the wilderness.

"There are many futures," Yarbrough said. His jubilant voice circled out of Ray's perception like water down the drain. *"You will have the greatest one of them all."*

Part Two
Ghost Radio

Thunder roared inside Ray's mind and trickled down through his skeletal structure into the ground under him. The very world shook apart, allowing him to glimpse down into the splitting existence beneath his feet. Deep in the earth, the core of the planet itself crumbled and broke, refashioning itself into a sort of black hole. The impossible infinity pried itself open to reveal a crack of pale light within its interior. His head flared with a migraine. Stabbing pressure pierced his brain, sending pain shockwaves reverberating into his very soul.

"*You aren't awake,*" Yarbrough said. "*Not yet.*"

Even though the boy couldn't see anything, Ray's numbed mind prevented fear from leaking out. He had the vague impression of still sitting in front of the radio beside his television, listening to the same fuzzed-out station he had been since around midnight. His off-kilter consciousness swirled, not quite connecting with his thoughts or attempts to move from his location. Every part of his being tilted slightly off-center. The world outside his rolled-back eyes remained as he remembered it, but an odd spiritual detachment kept him at arm's length from his surroundings.

"*We are usurpers of a future we deserve. Your parents lied, but don't blame them. They have never known Truth, and they never will. What you will hear from me is the real Truth. There is nothing else to tell.*"

The red sun peered through large office windows, shining against Ray's aching eyes. He rubbed at them in an attempt to focus. Just the fact that he could move, at least a little, allowed some relief to break through his sore muscles. Before him, a radio booth slid into focus, darkened without a single light inside the sealed small space. A man sat behind the glass at a desk, his lips whispering into the microphone before his shadowed face. Behind the figure, dusty and disheveled shelves lay coated in pale green brush and vines. Switchboards flashed in the dark under the plants. It was as if this place had been abandoned for decades and yet somehow remained operational.

The sandy-haired young man wore a plaid shirt and held a

clean-cut look. His eyes had black circles, the same ones in the album sleeve Lenny had given him. Yarbrough spoke into the microphone while staring out the scuffed window into the crimson sun.

"*Y Signal* is what I call it," the former rocker said. "Who I was no longer exists, just as the world you once knew is nothing but an illusion of things that *could* be. What *is* before you in that false world is nothing but a bad dice roll of uncaring chaos that ends in nothing. We can do better than that—I will do better than that. Forget about a new *tomorrow* when we can have a better *today*."

Ray's legs remained frozen to the torn-up red carpeting on the old wood floors. Warm air pushed against the back of the boy's neck, like from some busted air conditioner, and yet he couldn't look away from Yarbrough. It was as if his thoughts were being dragged into some sort of whirlpool beyond his comprehension.

The disheveled rocker stared beyond the boy as if speaking past him and into the blood-colored sun of this strange place. "I warned you about Oklahoma City, didn't I? Yet April came, and you did not heed my warning. Will you act on the bombings in Tel Aviv and Paris next month? How about Canada or Sri Lanka? I wonder. It is like you enjoy misery and death. I have offered to save you from the oncoming collapse, and yet all you do is sit there with static fuzzing in your wax-filled ears as the world detonates around you like a minefield. The Y Signal offers salvation. If you are ready to take that step, prepare yourself for the last train. It is arriving in mere hours! Be certain to answer the call or else be trapped here forever."

The boy opened his mouth to speak, but no voice projected from his throat. His brain flared in pain and the existence before him fuzzed in and out of focus. Was he even really awake? Hot air continued to press against the back of his head. The realization hit him that it wasn't air—it was breathing. Someone was standing behind him.

Ray's muscles seized, and he held his breath. Nonetheless, he couldn't turn away from the madman at the microphone.

"Who are you to argue?" Yarbrough continued. "You are just a possibility, a lucky flip of the coin. Your existence itself is as much mistake as it is fortunate—or unfortunate. You could just as easily be dead tomorrow with the rest of us when the world finally falls over like a poorly stacked house of cards. What the Y Signal has taught me is the path to the True Earth, the one we long-ago rejected for this lie we accept today. I will take you away from all of this, because it is what you deserve. Keep your dial tuned to this station, folks. Don't believe, just trust yourself. Soon enough, your deep knowledge will be rewarded. I'll make sure of it."

Ray bit the inside of his cheek. He needed some pain, some shock to the system to get him to move: anything to get away from the psycho sitting before him—and whatever was waiting at his back. Prickles of pain filled the inside of his mouth as Ray struggled against his invisible bonds. The hairs on his neck stood up straight with every movement he made. The aches allowed him to flinch.

A bulky hand clasped Ray's shoulder. The chill that bore into the boy's nerves finally handed him the energy to budge. Ray forced his arm to lash at his mystery attacker. He grabbed at the mysterious hand and felt . . . *fur*?

His stomach churned, but still he forced himself to act. Ray pried the thick fingers loose with his own trembling digits. The aggressor didn't fight him, even allowing the boy to spin around and face his aggressor. The instant he saw who it was, his blood chilled. It was not a man in a mask, but an eight-foot monstrosity of an ape-man.

Long hair adorned its crooked form, covering whatever pale face it might have in the dark black tangle. And yet inside that mess peeked the outline of something between the nostrils of a gorilla, the mouth of a thick-lipped human, and the dead eyes of a crazed mental patient. Humanity did not exist in this thing, but monsters weren't supposed to exist. And it was looking right at him.

The creature crouched as if readying to pounce, but the boy even couldn't so much as scream. He was going to die. Ray opened his mouth agape when the beast fell upon him.

The terrified child tripped backwards, his voice catching in his throat as his shaking legs gave out. The ape-man bore down into him, and Ray shut his eyes tight in response. The teeth tearing into his neck caused him to scream a voiceless scream.

Just before his life ended, the rouge sunlight flickered outside a window behind the hungry beast. A heavily shadowed, flapping giant beast swooped past the building, rattling the windows. As it flew by, its resulting screech signaled a being much larger than a mere bird.

But that sight didn't stop the ape-man. The jagged teeth

sunk into Ray's neck over and over, and Ray yelled bloody murder at his assailant. His very life drained from his broken body, and his corpse stilled on the dirty carpeting. Skin split and agony gripped his last bits of consciousness. Of all the places he would die, he never expected it to be in a hell-world like this.

His eyes watered as the pain and surrounding darkness enveloped him. The only question Ray could ponder as he slipped into death was why he ever turned that radio on in the first place. Pain left the boy to fade into death.

Somewhere nearby, Yarbrough laughed as the static signal cut out, leaving Ray dead in the void. The echo cut out, letting loose a low hum that gradually increased like feedback in an old amplifier. The seconds passed, and it rose to a fever pitch, breaking the numb thoughts in Ray's mind. Suddenly, the bonds on his mortality severed, allowing the boy a moment to react.

So he screamed.

Ray bellowed from his prone position and found the feeling return to his flesh. He fell back, as if the non-existent floor gave out under him, and felt the warm air of this Y Signal break out around him. The dark slowly peeled away to reveal muted light shining through something like stained glass. When he touched down against new ground, sparks of pain caused him to wake up.

"*Ray!*"

Chatter and organ music filled the formerly empty space. Ray opened his sore eyes and found the multicolored lights of the stained glass windows shining down upon him. He was alive?

The boy wiped the sweat from his eyes as his vision cleared up. Sun-heated linoleum cooled his back through his jacket coat, and the bright multicolored panes of stained glass pierced his rumbling headache. His parents, four-year-old brother, and other familiar adults, all sat in the pew beside his prone position. Only his mom and dad took note of him as the rest sang a hymn. Ray groaned and sat up off the floor, questioning just how he ended up in Church to begin with.

"*Ray!*" his father repeated. "What in the world is wrong with you? Stop playing around."

Queasiness bit at the boy's stomach, and his throat clenched. A hymn sang somewhere far in the back of his thoughts even though he could see the choir singing three rows over at the opposite end of the church. That faint buzz in his head quieted as the chanting knocked him awake. Had he been sleeping this whole time?

"I'm alive?" Ray asked. He slid into the pew beside his parents. "How?"

His father sighed. "Don't lie on the floor. Is this another silly game?"

"No, I . . ." Ray thought a moment. "Why am I in Church?"

The sea of men and women in suits and dresses had filled the Our Lady of Perpetual Help Church up tight as the choir sang their opening hymn. In the tangle, he found Andrew with his parents two rows ahead—but weren't his friend's parents coming home in the morning? Wait, was it morning *now*? But he didn't go to Church on Saturday. A few minutes ago it was Friday night. Wasn't he just in his room a minute ago? Ray rubbed his temples.

"Enough playing around, Ray," his mother whispered harshly in his ear. She nervously glanced around the pew as she spoke to her son. All of their neighbors seemed too busy singing to notice them. She leaned in on her son. "Not in Church!"

He looked at her like she was growing a second head out of her neck. "But I was just sleeping a second ago. I think."

"*Quiet!* Keep acting up and we're not getting Sunday McDonalds. You can play around later when no one else is watching, especially not the neighbors or the PTA." She rubbed his face with a tissue. "I thought I told you to you wash your face before we left?"

"It's Sunday?!" he rasped. Wooziness threatened to overtake the boy as his mother pocketed her tissue. It had been over 24 hours since he listened to the radio station? That wasn't possible. He couldn't have lost a whole day. "Don't joke around."

"Don't be fresh," she replied.

"I'm not." Even though his parents both wore their best Sunday clothes consisting of a cheap suit for his dad and a half-price floral dress for his mom, Ray couldn't help but think someone must be playing a joke on him. "I was just in my room a minute ago."

His father towered over him with his near-six foot height. "*Enough.* No playing games in Church. Is this because of what happened before we left? Did you overhear that phone call from Mrs. Crowe about the wastoid they arrested at the Radio Shack last night?"

For an instant, Ray saw the ape-man's ugly visage in his

father's disapproving glare and felt the color drain out of his face. He wiped at his forehead, trying to ignore the sweat dripping down his back. This wasn't a joke. Ray closed his eyes and pinched the bridge of his nose.

"The old bird is just paranoid about strangers, Ray. It's summer. You're going to see all sorts of weird characters around town. It doesn't make them all degenerates looking to cause trouble. The last thing we need is for them to think Burroughsvale is nothing but a bunch of crazies who can't keep their kids in line. Are you finished playing around now?"

Ray shook his head even as his stomach churned. "I'm fine."

"Good," his mom said. She feigned a smile to Ruth Johnson a row away while still whispering to Ray. "We don't need to talk about rumors in the church. You must behave. Everyone is looking."

"I have to go to the bathroom. Excuse me."

"Make it fast," his dad said.

Ray pushed his way out of the pew and dashed towards the rear end of the Church. The choir kept singing regardless, and the rest of the congregation went on as if nothing had happened. His mom was wrong: no one had even noticed him this entire time. He slipped down the stairs and white painted halls into the empty bathroom on the basement floor. The door closed behind him as he flew to the toilet. Thankfully, his retching only lasted about thirty seconds.

Muffled singing filled his aching ears as he stumbled out of the stall. The boy splashed sink water on his face and stared into the mirror. Try as he might he could not puzzle out just what had happened since he turned on the radio. What happened to Saturday? Blank pictures filled his hollowed-out memory like a bad roll of film.

Ray didn't look as disheveled as he felt in his Sunday clothes. His nicely creased navy blue pants, carefully slicked-back hair, and clean suit made him look like a lawyer on the prowl for his next ambulance. When his aunt saw him dressed like this she used to always ask the boy when the wedding was. But this was typical for a Sunday. What it didn't explain was why Ray didn't remember changing clothes in the first place. In fact, it still didn't explain missing a whole day of his life. Now he just had an overexposed movie reel rolling in his memory between turning on the radio and waking up in

Church. A day had disappeared.

That is, assuming any of this was real to begin with. The boy didn't discount the possibility that he still remained asleep. Was he imagining this moment right now? There was only one way to find out. He pinched his arm. Shockwaves of pain rippled through the skin on his wrist. Ray didn't rouse from any sleep.

"What in the world is going on?" he asked no one.

"That's what I'd like to know," Andrew replied.

Ray's heart nearly leaped through his chest at his friend's words. Andrew's combed-back hair and tan Sunday clothes never looked right on the taller boy, always slightly too short, but Ray's friend always did whatever his parents wanted—even if it was to wear terrible-fitting outfits. He might have been rowdy on the playground and on the streets, but when he was at home Andrew was always the model kid. A good actor for the 'rents. He was also creepily perceptive. Ray splashed some more water on his face while his friend leaned against the closed door.

Andrew tilted his head at his friend. "Your 'rents are freaking out and telling my folks you just had a bad headache, but I don't buy it. You've been weird since I called you last night."

"You called yesterday?" Ray watched his friend from the reflection in the mirror. "What did I sound like?"

"Normal, kinda. But it didn't sound like you were paying attention. Other things on your mind? Something happen at your grandma's place?"

"No, actually, I don't remember yesterday at all." Ray's tongue dried. He couldn't believe he had to admit that. The sick boy told his badly dressed friend about what he did after leaving the pizza parlor on Friday night. As he spoke, drops of memory splotched in his head as if they had always been there, like a heavy blanket slowly being peeled off of his warmed body. "I'm not sure if I just woke up a few minutes ago, or if my mind has been screwed up since I turned on that radio last night. It's insane."

Ray explained what he went through. It took a near minute of silence before Andrew managed to finally reply. His words arrived slowly and carefully. "I knew something was off! Your cousin was out of it, too. Do you remember? He looked like he had fallen out of bed. Then there was that weird punk hanging outside the pizzeria. How did he know about that Y Signal? This might have something to do with all the strange out-of-towners showing up around Burroughsvale. Have you heard from Lenny since Friday? I mean, if you can remember anything."

Ray stared at his friend in disbelief. Andrew had believed him so readily and completely that it was difficult to take in. Then again, Andrew was the one who swore by the existence of the Sasquatch and fairies. Weird stuff was his specialty. He would have gotten made fun of for it by everyone if he wasn't Andrew. Regardless, the shorter boy felt a bit of weight lift from his shoulders and sighed.

"No," Ray replied. The memories of his uneventful Saturday were now coming into view. "My grandma asked some questions about him, but that's all. No one's seen Lenny since we last saw him."

"We can fix that."

"I need to get over to his apartment." Ray's memories told him nothing that was out of the ordinary. All he found were typical events of every visit he had with his grandma over the years. But it wasn't himself he was worried about. What if something had happened to Lenny over the weekend, worse than what Ray had experienced? No one else understood this Y Signal, and they definitely wouldn't believe an eleven-year-old kid about it. "There's no way my 'rents will get any of this and let me go visit him right now, so it'll have to wait until after Church. I'll go home and get my bike."

"You can tell them we're going to spend some time at the arcade. Heck, if nothing's wrong with him, we'll make that the truth. Maybe this is all just a big old nothing, right? Shame the guys are busy today, but it is what it is."

The pair slid back into the Church as if nothing had happened. Ray's parents were none too happy he had skipped out on a hymn, never mind that he returned with Andrew, but they soon went back to paying attention to the reading before them. It was Church as normal, otherwise.

As he sat and listened about Elijah being taken up to Heaven in a whirlwind, he could only think about those strangely mundane memories returning to him. Ray had spent his Saturday baking with his grandmother, playing cards, and even learned a few canvas painting tips from her. It was not unlike any visit he had had with her before. Why had that broadcast prevented him from remembering it? He always enjoyed his time with her, and it was like it had been stolen.

A sinister notion caused his nerves to tighten: what if these memories were reruns? What if they were taken and rearranged from previous visits? What if they didn't actually happen yesterday but were just shoddy patchworks pulled together in his head? Maybe his mind had made it all up for his own benefit. Would he even know the difference? He did lose an entire day, after all.

As he sat through the Mass, it all unfurled in his head.

No, that wasn't it. Nothing that happened yesterday was taken from previous visits. His grandmother asked too many questions about Lenny's current weird state. Ray let out a deep breath. He had just sleepwalked through an entire day.

Ray had only experienced this broadcast the one time, and it did this much. He couldn't imagine what it might have done to someone like Lenny. That realization only strengthened Ray's resolve to visit him.

Why didn't Ray's own favorite cousin tell him about this Y Signal? Perhaps even he didn't know what was really happening with it. If more people stumbled into that midnight broadcast, then all kinds of chaos could be unleashed on Burroughsvale. Judging by the weird people popping up around town, maybe it already had.

When Church let out, Ray rushed home. He changed into a quick pair of jean shorts and clean ocean blue t-shirt, grabbed his Bart Simpson backpack, and planned the trek ahead of him. After thinking it through, Ray removed his bike from the backyard shed, locked the fence behind him, and took off down the street. The freshly pumped tires allowed a smooth ride across the warm pavement. It was nice to have something go right today.

Thankfully, his parents didn't say anything else about his odd behavior or ask him to explain himself. They had to take his little brother to a play-date or something about an advanced preschool and were running late. These days, it felt like they were giving the little guy more and more attention, bringing his bro to these weird parenting classes and programs, but it wasn't so bad. This left Ray free to roam town on his own. It was almost like being an adult.

Inside his father's sock drawer, he had found Lenny's spare apartment key. As long as he brought it back before the 'rents figured it out, everything would be copacetic. His dad probably forgot he even had it anyway. Not like he talked about Lenny much these days.

It was a humid Sunday, but not so bad on his bike and under the heavy maple branches shading the sunlight from the open neighborhood streets. A patchwork of lined shadows passed over him, shielding Ray from the thick air of summer. He wished he could enjoy it more as he pedaled through the sweltering day, but his mind was simply elsewhere.

Andrew soon joined his friend on his own bike, and then also took up the talking. "Like I thought, the other guys are a no-go. George is off camping already, and Danny's playing mini-putt with his family today. Not that they would have believed our story. I'm not sure how they could have made a difference if they came, anyway. Danny would just want to beat everything up and George would be shouting down all my ideas."

Ray sighed. "You can't do anything last minute during the summer, Andrew. You know that. Everyone has their own plans. Either way, we can't wait for them to free up their schedules. If Lenny is in trouble, I have to go now."

"Don't worry, man. I get it; I get it. I'm just sayin', it would have been nice to have some backup. Especially if we're dealing with a dead rock star."

"He's no star," Ray muttered.

The apartment wasn't too far, off St. Joseph Street where they last met on Friday. Lenny had told Ray's parents that he was planning on settling down in Burroughsvale. He would go on about how rock music was dying and would be completely corporate in a few years, and how the world would fall apart to match its death. Ray's parents thought he was just being his usually wacky self, running to the next adventure after the last, but Ray had seen it differently. His cousin had changed.

There was no more twinkle in Lenny's eye when he discussed far-off places or his plans for the future. Instead, he spoke in odd riddles and kept to himself. He was closing off, and no one had noticed. Even his father told Ray to let him be, that Lenny was just being his usual odd duck self, and the boy had listened. Now here he was, hurrying to Lenny's apartment. Did everyone have it wrong?

Andrew was already off his bike and running for the building foyer before Ray reached the sidewalk. St. Hubert Street was always oddly quiet in both the summer and on the weekends, despite literally being located across from Mary Gardner Elementary where most local kid sports teams played and the Boy Scouts met. And yet most of the time, there was nobody to be seen on the streets. Even the relatively small apartment building before them was completely quiet.

Ray always had the impression that he was being watched on this street, despite the silence. It was a small area, but it felt smaller than it looked. No one even sat on their balconies or loitered around their windows in any of these apartment buildings. It wasn't unlike a ghost town despite the sunny weather and the distant rumble of engines around the circumference of the area. That the center of town could be so quiet was a little unnerving.

"Come on, Ray." Andrew waved him into the foyer, and Ray quickly joined his impatient friend. "Awesome, it's cool in here!"

"You're too excited," Ray said. "Lenny won't open up if you sound too eager. Calm it down."

"What a suspicious weirdo. No wonder he got in with the crowd that did *that* to you. He's missing a few screws."

"Ease up. Lenny's a good guy. He's always been a wanderer, at least that's what my dad said. If we can help him get away from these creeps, then that's good. But before any of that junk, I need to know what that Y Signal thing actually is. If it messed with me that badly, then I can't even imagine what it did to *him*. He's also had that nut-bag Yarbrough's very own radio for years now. Who knows what else he might have of his."

Andrew pointed to the button panel beside the sealed front door. "Which one am I buzzing?"

The numbers listed by the locked door into the building had a name by each button. Every listing was arranged by the floor and apartment number. However, Lenny's name had yet to be added to the plate with the others. Ray had asked him why that was, but he never received an answer. Lenny didn't explain much of anything these days. After that broadcast, Ray was beginning to understand why his cousin might not want people to know where he was.

The two boys buzzed apartment 310. Lenny always took his time answering, so Ray waited thirty seconds before pushing the button again. He repeated the process three times before Andrew tapped his shoulder.

"I think he's out, man."

"One second, let me think." Lenny wouldn't be out this

early in the day, never mind on a Sunday. There had to be another explanation. Unfortunately, the ones he thought up were not pleasant. "What if he's unconscious or hurt? I'm going to buzz someone else and see if they'll let me in to check."

Ray pressed the button for apartment 107, and an answer came not even two seconds later in a burst of static. An old man on the other end asked for a name. The boy calmly reintroduced himself to the landlord.

"Yeah, I remember you," the gruff voice said. "He should be in. Go right on up."

The lock let out an atonal howl that echoed off the badly plastered white walls of the foyer. Ray swung the door open and charged into the barren lobby and up the stairs. Andrew tore in after him. The annoying sound finally departed when the door clicked closed behind them.

Andrew groaned. "If he's in, then why didn't he answer?"

"We're about to find out." Ray showed Andrew the apartment key before slipping it back into his pocket. "Either way, we're going to learn something today. Hopefully, it's good."

The pair pushed through the empty white halls towards the staircase at the end of the long, narrow pathway. The sterile faded grey carpeting looked thin with loose strands sticking up, but it was otherwise the only thing aside from the pale yellow lighting to guide their way. Even as they walked the hallway, there were no sounds from any of the neighboring apartments. Ray would have believed this building completely vacant had he not been in here before. That knowledge didn't prevent a warning bell from jangling inside his numbed brain.

A clatter of echoing footfalls bounced off the vacant steel railing and the metal steps of the stairway. Someone else was in this cramped space with them. Ray couldn't discern whether the party was above or below but walked on regardless. There was no sense attracting unwanted attention, especially since they weren't actually residents.

As they rounded the bend to the second floor, a flood of steps from above revealed a tall young man coming down. He wore a pale yellow band t-shirt and had unkempt dreadlocks that fell down to his torn jean shorts. Ray recognized him as the mumbling punk from outside the pizzeria on Friday. He looked like one of the guys on the back of those skate-punk albums Lenny used to show him. Fashion was bizarre in Southern California, and this guy looked like he could barely dress himself. But this punk's cracked teeth, half-open brown eyes, and unevenly tanned skin, made him look as if he were only half-awake. Mutters escaped from his jagged breath as he shuffled down the steps, passing Ray and Andrew. He glanced at them once but said nothing in his descent.

Andrew elbowed his friend, and the two kept climbing up. There was no sense lingering.

On the third floor, the two boys reached apartment 310. Ray stuck the key in the lock and easily opened it. Finally, they could abandon those eerie hallways for a safer place. The pair pushed inside before Ray turned back and locked them inside.

"Why did you do that?" Andrew asked.

"In case that guy comes back."

"You think he will?"

Ray rolled his eyes. "Duh! Of course, I do."

"You don't know what he was doing in the building. Heck, he probably just left."

"He knew about the Y Signal, and he said Lenny's name the other day. That's enough for me."

Lenny's apartment had been left untouched, as if he just walked out of it seconds ago. The couch and coffee table sat clean in their usual spot on top of the grey carpeting. His NES video game console and controllers lay neatly on top of his old television set. Ray remembered playing old games with his favorite cousin on this thing ages ago. Good times. Everything here was as it should be. And yet, despite the cleanliness, an ineffable feeling scratched at Ray's spinning thoughts.

He rushed down the left hall towards the bedroom. "Lenny? Are you alright?"

At the back of the apartment, he passed the bathroom and then the two bedrooms. Ray had already helped his cousin move in here, so he knew what they looked like but still found their well-polished shelves and vacuumed floors off-putting. Even the record collection had been organized alphabetically with everything in its correct spot in the second bedroom. Nothing but old instruments, including a drum-set, filled the closet in that room. For dressing like a disheveled-looking mess, Lenny unquestionably kept a clean pad.

Lenny's bed had been made, and the clothes closet organized right, even if it was also filled with heavy boxes of vinyl records and radio parts. The only thing that felt out of place was the old radio on the nightstand. A strange aura of malice wafted off of the dirty plastic and busted tape deck of the small object. It otherwise looked like any cheap junk you could find at the mall. Was this the one Yarbrough had given him?

"What in the world happened?" Ray asked no one. "What is going on in this town?"

Ray inspected the drawers and found what appeared to be poetry or lyrics. Words and statements about uncertainty and dread for the future. No notes or any kind of journal existed, just his cousin's usual attempts at art. Boxes were also jammed under the bed frame so tightly that he couldn't even remove them to see what they contained. Nothing else of interest had been left here.

Then there was that radio—the one Lenny had supposedly received from Yarbrough himself, or at least from his will after he disappeared a few years ago. It wasn't that new, but the radio tuner was set on a familiar station: 99.9. It was the same station that had poisoned Ray's mind. Perhaps Lenny had listened to the exact same broadcast the boy had that night. Perhaps he didn't escape it. The likelihood of that possibility caused Ray's breaths to sharpen.

Just the look of this cheap radio bothered the boy a good deal. He thought of distant lands of evil ape-men and wild pseudo-dinosaurs or whatever other madness Yarbrough had shoved into Ray's brain. Whatever might have happened—this radio couldn't be left here. Not if it might contain some clue to where Lenny or that ex-rocker disappeared to. Ray unplugged it and carried the surprisingly light object under his arm. When he got back to the safety of his home, he would inspect it there. Right now, the idea of staying in this place caused his knees to shake.

In the living room, he met his friend who had just emerged from the kitchen. Despite the fact that they were alone, Ray kept getting the idea they were being watched. All the more reason to get out of that place as soon as possible.

Andrew scratched his freshly scuffed-up hair and sighed. "Even the fridge was cleaned and emptied. Your cousin is definitely a weirdo. What's with the radio?"

"This is Yarbrough's. It's the one he gave it to Lenny after he disappeared a few years ago, probably for being such a good roadie. I don't know what it has to do with any of this, but it has to be some sort of key to why this is happening." He glanced at the phone beside the couch. Suddenly, a memory of Lenny's words popped into his thoughts. Ray handed the radio to Andrew. "Hold this for a second."

A small red book had been left under the phone. Most of the pages had large scribbling which crossed out names and numbers. Ray followed them towards the back of the cheap address book. This had been carefully gone through alphabetically, and probably recently. Who was Lenny calling up?

That thought caused him to pause. Who was it that Lenny asked him to contact when they spoke on Friday? He craned his neck in thought. Some guy named Billy? But that wasn't a last name. Ray flipped through the book, searching for this mystery man. Lenny wouldn't have told his cousin that name without a reason.

"I don't want to alarm you, Ray," Andrew whispered. He was staring out the window by the balcony door. "But I think that punk from before is looking at our bikes."

Ray didn't look up as he flipped through the tiny phone book. Billy's full name and number had to be here. The punk no longer concerned him. "Why would he do that?"

"Oh, man. He's looking up here!"

"What?!"

Ray pocketed the address book and joined his friend at the window. The punk was standing exactly where Andrew had said he was, standing over their bikes. His oblong right hand shielded his eyes from the sun as he glanced up into the apartment. He was looking for something, or someone. As Ray looked the wiry man over, the punk pointed to Lenny's apartment and shouted something that couldn't be heard from their location on the third floor. Whatever he said probably wasn't anything children needed to hear.

The door behind them banged as if an elephant had charged into it. The boys choked on their voices before they spun around to meet it. On the other side of the locked door, someone swore.

"Who's in there? Is that Lenny?" a meaty voice growled. "Open the door before I open *you* up. Where is the Y Signal?"

This voice repeated the same words in a weirdly repetitive manner, like a chant. It definitely wasn't the landlord.

Down on the first floor, the punk had already sprinted back towards the building. He was coming back in.

And he was heading this way.

The apartment door bent and rattled against the weight of whoever was behind it. This other psychopath would be inside within minutes. The boys had no way to escape.

Andrew ran for the phone. He picked it up and swore. "It's dead! Doesn't your cousin pay his bills?"

"There's got to be an exit," Ray said. He almost thought of hiding, but the packed rooms in Lenny's place made that impossible. They really only had one option, and he didn't relish choosing it.

There was no escape from the third floor, and none of the neighbors appeared to care about what was happening. That is, if there *were* any neighbors. Ray quickly shook that insane notion away. He thought for a second. There actually was one way out, but Andrew wouldn't like it. To be honest, Ray *himself* didn't like it. The idea was just insane, but they had no other option.

Ray swallowed the trembling fear in his voice and forced a shaky smile at his friend. "The balcony."

The door rattled again, and a crack split across the center of the frame. This mental patient would not be deterred from his prize.

Andrew squeaked under his breath. "The balcony? You want us to go out by the third-floor balcony? Are you insane?"

"I saw the closets. There's no room to hide in them. Lenny was also dumb enough to stuff boxes under the bed. Where else do we go? You want to tell that psychopath to go away instead?"

"But *the balcony*? I'll ask again: are you insane?"

"Only one way to find out," Ray said. He opened the door to the small balcony and spied the barren street of St. Hubert three stories below. Aside from a few untrimmed conifer trees in the gap between this building and the one to their left, he saw nothing that would remotely break a potential fall—and even those trees were about thirty feet out of reach. The two boys were alone on the third floor. Perhaps, this idea really was too crazy to work. "Oh boy."

Ray gathered what little courage he had left and moved his shaking knees onto the balcony. He couldn't even imagine jumping off the high dive in the community pool, and yet here he was like some *MacGyver* wannabe. Nonetheless, there was little choice left. Scaling the balcony down three floors remained the only alternative to certain death. The boy placed the radio and small phone book in his Bart Simpson backpack. Andrew joined him outside and shut the balcony door behind them. The front door bent and cracked with the force of whoever was out there pounding on it.

"Okay," Ray said to his friend. He swore and rubbed his temples. "Just don't look down."

"Looking isn't going to stop me from hitting the ground and breaking my stupid neck, Ray. But I guess we have no choice, huh? I'm going to have nightmares for years if we get out of this."

The shouts and creaking wood only sang louder back inside the apartment. That nut would definitely break in at any second. The boys had no further option. Drop down or die.

Ray put his leg over the third-floor balcony and took a hard breath. His limb trembled as he fought the urge to look down at his potential death. It was now or never. He nodded to his friend and laughed a nervous laugh. All of this was because of that stupid Y Signal.

"If I ever see Lenny again," Ray said, "I'm going to punch him right in the mouth."

Part Three
Blindsided

Ray descended the third-floor balcony first, his backpack rattling behind him with the radio and notebook safely inside. His muscles strained, but it wasn't any worse than climbing the many backyard fences around town—as long as he didn't look down. Andrew waited above him as patiently as he could despite someone pounding on the apartment door inside. They didn't have the time to play it safe. Ray tried ignoring it all as he carefully shimmied down the bars towards the second floor.

Thankfully, the metal bars were sturdy despite their thin nature. They allowed the boy to slide down and clasp his fingers on the bottom of the old grey platform. The cheap paint stained his fingers as his feet kicked for the top railing of the second-floor balcony under him. Being eleven was only a real pain when your short stature came into play—like it did at this very moment. Ray stretched, doing his best to avoid looking down at certain death. His feet dangled underneath him as he swung forward.

"What's wrong?" Andrew whispered from above. "Don't tell me you're too short?"

"Shut up! I don't need this right now."

"Calm down and pay attention, Ray!"

There was no time to doubt himself. Ray needed to make a gamble before his arms gave out and he met the earth below with his face. He swung himself back and forth. Warm air and sunlight brushed the back of his neck, but his sweating fingers were a bigger concern. On his third movement, he pitched forward with all his strength and soared over the railing.

He landed hard on the balcony and his head smacked into the bars on the opposite side. Blurry flashes of red light caused him to roll on his knees. Sweat dripped across his eyes as he wiped them clean. Did he really just climb down to the second floor?

Scuffling shoes landed beside him. Ray looked up as Andrew checked his friend's certainly bruised forehead.

"You alright?" Andrew asked.

"Just need the buzzing in my brain to stop then I'll be good. You're fast, by the way."

"I've done stupider things before. We should keep going before someone sees us out here."

"Wait a second. Did you hear that?"

Cracking wood brought Ray's attention back to the floor above them. Men shouted in the apartment that the boys had just abandoned. Ray could swear he heard furniture smashing and breaking. Had a fight broken out?

"This Lenny gave me the slip last month, but not this time," someone said. "Last night's broadcast said tonight is the last chance. Tell me where you're hiding him. The Y Signal is mine."

A reedier voice grumbled. "You haven't been chosen. I can tell by your smell. You belong in a dumpster, not paradise."

"Say that to my face, psycho!" A loud thump echoed out of the apartment. "How about I fix your face to look as ugly as the rest of you?"

"*Ray!*" Andrew whispered. "Hurry up before they look out on the balcony. I don't think they were searching for us, but I still don't want them to see us out here. They're here for that Y Signal you were talking about."

They actually wanted this thing? These punks wanted to get in on whatever madness Lenny had gotten himself into. They wouldn't be so interested if they had any clue as to what that Y Signal was.

Or perhaps they *did*. Perhaps it was Ray that was missing the truth to this whole thing. After all, he only entered Yarbrough's world once. He might have missed something when he was there. Sure, it hurt, but was it really so bad? A warm nostalgia bathed his mind. He hadn't seen everything. Maybe if Ray visited that place a second time . . .

"*Ray!*" Andrew repeated.

Ray rubbed the bridge of his nose to fight off the growing migraine. What was he thinking? The boy exhaled a deep breath. "What do we do now?"

"The apartment this balcony belongs to is locked. I swear, no one lives in this stupid building. We need to head down again, and we gotta do it faster. You gonna be okay?"

"I don't have a choice. We can't let them get this radio."

"The radio? I just don't wanna die. What does that radio have to do with anything?"

Ray didn't know, but a small voice buried in his jumbled thoughts told him to hold onto that stupid trinket no matter what happened. It was the only clue he had left to find Lenny, aside from that address book. All he needed to do was get past the first-floor balcony and survive the short drop to the ground floor. That should be easy enough! At least, he needed to tell himself it was. If he stopped to think about the insanity of what he was actually doing his guts would give out on him.

Ray swung down on the balcony bars towards the next platform. He gripped onto the metal, his arms burning. The first floor was just ahead. This time, Ray wasted little time finding his footing and touching down on the solid balcony. Just the ground level remained.

Andrew descended on the opposite side and found his footing beside him. "Almost there!"

Shouts and crunching in the apartment above caused Ray to pause as he held onto the bars. The boy chanced a glance back up while he was still steadying himself for the jump.

The punk stared down at him from the top-floor balcony. His sunken eyes glared at the two boys. Blood stained his bruised cheeks and his fat lip. He said nothing before swooping back into the apartment like a vampire.

"That freak's coming down!" Ray said.

Andrew glanced around madly. "Who's coming?"

"The gross guy we saw on the stairs. We need to get to our bikes and get out of here." Ray wasted no time bracing himself on the railing again. The ground was easily over ten feet down and wouldn't be a comfortable landing. He might even break something, or worse. There wasn't much of a choice if he wanted to get away. "I'm making a leap for the grass. Once I land, I'm going right for the bikes. We need to make it quick."

"Wait a second, Ray!"

But he couldn't. There was something in the way that punk stared at them in the hall and from the balcony that made it seem as if a piece of this guy was missing. That psycho wanted to catch them because they had what he wanted. Whatever that something *was* didn't matter. All Ray knew was that he had to get away quick.

So he did.

Ray bounded off the first-floor balcony. The summer sun

baked his aching bones as he soared downwards and braced himself for a hard landing. Just before touching the grass, he hit it sideways in a roll. His backpack jiggled in his spin, rattling madly. He hoped the radio didn't break in his frantic momentum. Stings of red pain rippled across Ray's arms and knees leading him to yelp as he flew across the grass off-kilter.

His sore legs trembled as he scrambled to stand back up. That fall hurt more than he let on, but he still had to get to his bicycle before that punk reached the bottom floor. Ray quickly regained his balance and flew towards the bikes lying on the walkway ahead of him.

A thud distracted him. Andrew shouted from behind.

Ray chanced a glance back. Andrew rolled on the grass like a fish out of water. Ray's friend slowly climbed to all fours, struggling to stand. A turtle on its back wouldn't have looked more awkward than Andrew did at that moment in the middle of the grass. Ray rushed to his friend's side, his ribs burning under the strain.

"My ankle won't move right," Andrew said. "I think I twisted it."

"Grab my shoulder. We just gotta get to the bikes, and we can make tracks."

The boys leaned against each other in their stumbling steps, moving much slower than Ray wanted them to. In any second, he expected the punk to burst out of the entranceway in a furious rage. It wouldn't be so bad if it didn't seem like this entire neighborhood was completely vacant, meaning that he couldn't even be sure anyone would come if they called for help. No one had heard the banging upstairs or had seen the two boys climb down to the ground floor, after all. Not even the landlord appeared to be there. Was he just a figment of Ray's imagination? No, Andrew had also heard him. Hopefully he at least called the cops. Still, it was like only the two kids existed in this world aside from the crazies chasing them. Ray pushed ahead with Andrew leaning on him, his mind on the bikes. He didn't want to think about this anymore.

His tall friend groaned and swore with every awkward lope forward. Sweat poured down Ray's neck as his muscles twisted with his jerky movements. Why did it feel like he was moving through molasses? Andrew stumbled over to his bike and wobbled onto the seat. Ray did the same. A scream pitched out of the silent neighborhood from behind him. He knew the source without looking back.

"*Hey!*"

The punk ran out of the entranceway, his own legs wobbling like he had seen the front end of a Buick in rush hour. Ray cursed his luck and pedaled. This guy was too fast, despite his very obvious injuries.

Andrew shouted between clenched teeth as he tore out onto the road. Luckily, his injured ankle didn't keep him from biking. Ray followed after his injured friend, away from the building. They blitzed down the barren street, their speed a little sluggish at first before they forced their legs to pedal like they hadn't before. The pair looked back only once.

The punk stood in the middle of the road, his formerly pale face a shade of red as he watched the two boys ride down the street and out of sight. All Ray could think about was where the other guy banging on the upstairs apartment had gone. Ray let the concern fade and focused on the road ahead. The bloody punk soon faded from memory as they turned off St. Hubert Street.

The two boys rode down the road, Andrew falling back to let Ray take the lead. His face paled sheet white. Wherever they were going had to be a place they wouldn't be followed to, and hopefully be alone in. Ray's friend needed to rest, and he needed a plan.

"The mall," Ray said. "We go in through the park and into the back entrance. No one drives through there. We can lose anyone who might be tailing us, and we can decide what to do next."

"If you say so, dude. My ankle is killing me. I just want to sit and take a breather."

They pedaled off down the small slope back towards St. Joseph Street. Cars blitzed past the four-way intersection as the duo waited at the stop sign. Ahead lay two possible destinations: the park in one direction and the mini-mall from Friday in the other. The mini-mall wouldn't have enough cover: they needed to head for the real deal. Traffic was a bit busier than Ray expected but not enough to throw off anyone potentially following them. Getting out of sight was the priority.

When the break in traffic came, the pair crossed the street and traveled left down the sidewalk towards the park. More apartment buildings met them in their journey, as did a familiar convenience store. The two turned between the buildings and rolled down a gravel path beyond recently trimmed overhanging brush into the park. Lush shrubs and old park benches met them as they glided through the stifling summer day.

It wasn't a big park, though it was certainly an active one. At least two dozen kids climbed the jungle gym, running around in circles like wild apes. They hopped on the benches and swayed with the large swing sets in their own mad rhythms. This lot appeared to be part of some sort of playgroup from Centennial Elementary or the preschool as Ray didn't recognize any of them. Nonetheless, the pair rode past the crowd towards their destination. At least, they would make good cover.

Across from the park, they rode up a steep dirt hill through a torn fence opening into the parking lot. Dirt kicked up under their tires as they wheeled to the rear entrance of the mall. Ray and Andrew glided towards the bike rack and took a deep breath when they realized they were alone.

The duo parked their bicycles. The barren back-lot allowed them to sit at one of the two picnic tables placed by the lone line of parked cars. Most of the people who came here used the lot in front of the mall which meant privacy for anyone who came through this way. The thick line of brush on one side, and a large building on the other definitely helped not being seen. The two boys took advantage as they finally allowed themselves to breathe. Andrew rubbed his right ankle and Ray let his lungs catch up with the rest of him. It took about a minute before either spoke again.

"Put your ankle up, Andrew. You don't want that sprain to get worse."

"I've *had* worse." Andrew complied with his friend's wishes by sitting on the shaded grass and placing his leg up on the bench of the table. "It's not that bad, but I could use some ice."

"Got any money?" Ray asked. "I don't have much left since the movie on Friday."

"I have a couple of bucks. Not enough for a . . . compress? Is that what it's called?"

"Well, I was thinking I'd get ice from the food court. I've barely got enough change, though."

Andrew handed Ray a few dollar bills. "Keep the change. I'm not going anywhere ever again. Not after today."

"I'll be right back." Ray took out Lenny's red book and nodded to his prone friend. "Stay still."

"Funny guy."

The book burned in Ray's torn-up palms as he walked towards the entrance. He flipped open the pages trying to see if he recognized any names. That was difficult to do while he weaved through the packed crowds of the mall. This place was always packed on the weekends, and today was no different.

He had been to this mall hundreds of times, but it wasn't all that impressive. Ray had visited so many of these things while on vacations and on cross-country trips with his extended family that he knew just how lame this one actually was. The Burroughsvale Mall was really just a glorified hallway with far too many boring clothes stores.

But it didn't bother him. Since Burroughsvale wasn't that big to begin with, neither was the mall. This building was comprised of a single floor that only had a thin row of stores along each side of a lone hall. It stretched about half a block, but for this town, it was enough. The main attraction was the Woolworths that closed back when he was in third grade, but kids still poured in for the food court and the arcade at lunch and after school—the place being down the street from his own elementary school and the bigger school for the older kids probably helped.

"Hey, Ray, tell your mom I said hi!" a middle-aged woman said as he walked by. He waved back to her as he slipped through the crowd. Vera Tracey was apparently out with her two kids, checking the dollar store like she usually did. "Have a good day!"

This was June, summer vacation, which meant the flood of younger people and their mothers didn't surprise him. They walked the mall, swarming in and out of the bookstore, the Electronic Boutique video game establishment, and even the pet shop. Ray didn't have time for any of that today.

The food court in the Burroughsvale Mall was more or less a circle with a cache of tables littered in the center. Most of the stores were packed, leading him to believe it must have been around lunchtime, though without his watch he couldn't be sure. He approached the Pizza Barn and waited behind a teenage couple, a sixth grader he hardly recognized outside of school, and a granny in a floral shirt and done-up grey hair. The chatter in this place was oddly soothing, contrasting against the quiet of Lenny's place and the static of the radio broadcast that stuck to him like dried sweat.

For once, he could think of summer vacation and how things would soon go back to normal again. The sun, the happy faces, and the bustling activity, reminded him that the world really was a place of hopeful energy and smiles like Mom had said. He could finally forget about the Y Signal. Hey, wasn't that Kristin Oliver over at the pet shop? Maybe he could—

"*Does the number nine-eleven mean anything to you? It should, because it means something to those who wish you dead.*"

Ray blinked. He scanned over the crowded food court. No one was using the speaker system. Where did that voice come from?

"*Do you get it yet, listeners? Yugoslavia is going to be blown to bits! A Canadian terrorist is going to blow up a Montreal bus next year. A falling satellite is going to crush a small village outside of Dusseldorf. Wait until you see what a simple flu will do to Hong Kong. The world is over. You can't go back to your normal life and pretend it's all okay. It's not! It's a lie. But you know this, whether you want to accept it or not. The last train rolls in tonight. Will you board it?*"

"Oh no," Ray whispered. It was Yarbrough. The voice played overhead as if projecting through the PA system, but no one else appeared to hear it. They just went on doing what they always did, munching on their lunches and chatting away about summer reruns and sports. Why was it that only Ray was being subjected to this? Maybe he was just going mad. "Please, just go away already."

"*I have the way out—the way out of the oncoming Armageddon. Follow me there. Tonight, we take the last train home.*"

"Where are you?" Ray asked.

"Hey, kid," the cashier said. The middle-aged fat woman stared down at him from behind the counter, her large fingers tapping on a plastic tray. She wore a green cap and matching apron with the Pizza Barn logo on it and looked like she wanted to be anywhere else. "Are you gonna order or what?"

Ray shook the rattling thoughts of doomsday from his head. "Sorry, ma'am."

After being handed the cup and the pizza slice on a paper plate, Ray paid the annoyed woman and slunk out of the food court. He made a beeline back out of the mall towards his injured friend, ignoring the living world around him. He couldn't deal with this. Not now. Yarbrough's voice had disappeared, but Ray's mind began to twist in weird ways.

The boy remembered odd visits with Lenny where he would talk about old food places that hadn't existed since the older cousin was a kid himself. How they would come up, do well, vanish, and never be heard from again. It seemingly happened overnight. Names like G. D. Ritzy, Gino's Hamburgers, and Wag's, which Lenny had discovered in his many journeys all disappeared from the collective consciousness. Sometimes, he wondered if they ever really existed to begin with when no one else remembered them. Perhaps none of this was real. Now Ray questioned if he was experiencing the same thing. But that was crazy, right? Lenny was just the black sheep.

Nonetheless, he couldn't help but ponder on it. Did that mean all these places Ray knew so well might one day go away as well?

Ray fought the urge to look back at the food court. It would be there the next time he returned, and it always would be here in Burroughsvale, no matter how much time had passed. Lenny was just being weird, and it was rubbing off on his exhausted cousin. Once they found that jerk, this would all get straightened out. Nothing was ending tonight. The world would go on, same as it always did, and always would. Things changed, sure, but that didn't mean they went away. Progress can't just cast things aside or else it isn't progressing to anything. People would never forget what mattered, how else would they learn? His mother always said so. She never steered him wrong. Parents knew everything, much as he hated to admit it.

Outside, Ray handed Andrew his paper plate and drink. Andrew dumped the soda and wrapped the ice in the paper plate. He kept his ankle elevated as he held the ice over his sock. Ray's friend attempted to give him back the slice of pizza, but when Ray refused he ended up shoving the piece into his own mouth. It was just as well. Andrew needed the energy right now, not him.

"Did you get to take a look through the book?" Andrew asked between bites.

"No, I was a bit . . . distracted."

"Better late than never, bud. Give it a look. We have all the time in the world."

"Maybe not."

"What do you mean?"

"Never mind. Let me get it out."

45

Ray dug into the book and poured through the names. He didn't know any of these people, and, at this point, wasn't even convinced they existed, or if anything did, and yet he was certain this Billy character that Lenny mentioned on Friday had to be in there. Lenny didn't lie, even if he was insane. Eventually, Ray reached the only promising name. William Thwombly was listed beside a nickname that read *Spikes*. Ray traced the number with his finger.

While Andrew finished up his slice, Ray entered the phone booth beside the mall's rear entrance and dialed the number. The small space smelled like wet dog and skunk, but these things always stunk. He held his nose and waited for someone to pick up.

The phone clicked on the fourth ring, and a deep voice spoke on the other end. "*Who is it?*"

"Is this Spikes?"

"*No. I'm an adult, and this is 1995, kid. I don't go by that name anymore.*"

"I'm Ray. This is about my cousin Lenny. He said Billy wanted an update. Is that you?"

A pause on the other end caused Ray's breath to stiffen. For a second, he thought he had been disconnected, losing his only living lead. Billy made a strange sound that could have been considered a cough and sucked on his teeth. It felt like an eternity before he spoke again. "*I'll give you my address. Make sure no one follows you.*"

After scribbling down the address this Spikes guy gave him, Ray didn't even have the chance to ask another question before Billy told him not to call again and hung up. Whoever this guy was, paranoia was his middle name.

Andrew waited by the picnic table for his friend to return. He kept the ice on his ankle as he sat there, nodding his head to an invisible beat. "I take it that you didn't get anything?"

"No, I did. It's just . . . it was weird. That guy sounded bored and annoyed until I mentioned my cousin. Then it was like he got a shot in the arm."

"Lenny has some strange friends. Makes sense, since he's a nut-job. Are we going?"

"No other choice. I'm not risking a ride back home just yet. Those guys might still be out there waiting around St. Hubert. Whoever they were. We should stay away from that part of town for now. No one's at home, anyway."

"That means this guy doesn't live near your cousin? I don't want to go across town again."

"He lives right over there, man."

The directions Billy gave were fairly straightforward. In fact, they led back to one of the apartment buildings beside the very park they passed through. Ray appreciated the short distance since Andrew wouldn't need to move as much. The last thing Ray wanted to do was leave his friend alone or send him back home with those creeps somewhere out there. Leaving Andrew injured, defenseless, and on his own would be a punk move. Lenny would have looked down on him, too.

It only took two minutes to ride over to the apartment just behind the park. None of the kids reacted to their return if they even remembered who they were to begin with, which made slipping into the building as easy as a free credit game at the arcade. Andrew hobbled a bit after him. Ray's friend had quite the poker-face when he wanted one.

"You okay, Andrew?"

"Ankle's not swollen. I'm good. I just want to keep off of it."

Ray hit the buzzer at the front door, and it clicked open almost instantly. Had this Billy guy been waiting since he called? Ray hoped this might be a sign that they would get in and out of there quick. He'd had enough running around for one summer, even if it was still early in the season.

Billy's apartment was thankfully on the first floor, which meant a short walk. They crossed the small atrium of wide-open black stairs and matching potted plants on either side. It was cheaper looking than Lenny's building, yet it felt somewhat livelier with the sounds of squawking kids and Sunday afternoon movies playing off too loud televisions. Having the park behind the building and a busy street nearby probably helped to liven this area up. Nonetheless, the duo only had to travel two doors over from the entrance before they reached the right apartment.

When Ray knocked on the door he wasn't that surprised to see it answered so fast. No, he was far more surprised by the man who answered it.

Billy was surprisingly short, though with a bit of muscle under his too-long t-shirt and torn jean shorts. He was not that much taller than the two boys. The long dark hair draping his face made it hard to see his green eyes under the mop. They looked somewhat unfocused as if they hadn't been allowed rest in far too long. He scratched the stubble on his chin as he looked them over.

"Take me to the radio," Billy said.

"Well," Ray began. He debated with himself about telling the truth. He decided finding his cousin mattered more than testing his wits against Lenny's friends. "I have it on me."

"Even better," Billy replied. "We don't have a lot of time if we want to catch up with Lenny."

Ray and Andrew followed Lenny's friend into the one-bedroom apartment. The blinds were drawn so the lack of sunlight made visibility rough. Not that it mattered since he only had a chair and a couch in the living room beside a pair of small tables. The boys sat down on the bigger piece of furniture, and Billy fell into the small chair by the darkened window.

"Do you have an ice-pack?" Andrew asked. "Not to be a jerk, but I could use one for my foot."

"Sure." Billy departed into the kitchen with relative quickness. He shuffled around a drawer and the freezer for a few seconds before he emerged with the ice pack and some cubes in a small plastic bag. Lenny's friend handed them to Andrew. "Might want to sit on the floor and put that ankle up. Sorry, kid. This ain't the Ritz."

"Why are you called *Spikes*, Billy?" Ray asked. "I don't see any on you."

"My hair used to be up, and a different color. That was back when we . . . it's ancient history, kid. How do you know who I am? I asked Lenny never to tell anyone I was in this nowhere town. He mentioned this place he grew up in so many times back in the day, and somehow, I still moved here before he did. No idea why he waited so long to tell me about this Y Signal business either."

Ray tried his best to explain everything since his wild Friday night, from the meeting with Lenny, to the dream, to escaping the apartment not even hours ago. Even though he experienced it himself, it was very hard to accept what actually occurred as reality. A part of Ray insisted he just had some sort of intense fever brought on by staying up too late, but a bigger part of him knew that definitely wasn't true. The Y Signal had to have some kind of answer for this.

Billy stared at Ray with half-closed lids. The disheveled man's eyes nearly rolled back in his head. It was as if he was simultaneously enthralled and bored. He was definitely Lenny's friend.

When the pesky kid finished, Spikes stood up from his chair. "Bring out the radio, boys."

Ray and Andrew exchanged glances. He believed this nonsense all too easily. Ray's friend cleared his throat. "For what?"

"You'll see. Set it up. I'll be right back."

The man formerly known as Spikes slunk into his bathroom and closed the door. Ray did what Billy told them to and set up the radio on the small table by the window. While he reached down to plug it in, a buzzing sound screeched from Billy's bathroom. A shaver? Ray tried to put this weirdo out of his mind and remind himself why he was there to begin with.

Andrew watched the radio like a mouse watches a house cat. "Didn't you say that the Y Signal has to wait until after midnight?"

"Yes," Ray said. "I thought he knew that. He is Lenny's friend, after all. The guy looks a bit out there, but Lenny always ran with an odd crowd. He is the black sheep, remember?"

"This psychopath doesn't even have any pictures up on his wall or books or movies or any shelves to put them on. It's like he just moved in here yesterday. We should just leave, man. Are you sure you saw what you think you saw on Friday night? Maybe you just ate a bad clam or whatever."

"No," Ray replied. He finished propping the radio beside the window before he continued. "I thought I might be crazy, but there is too much happening at once. Why was that punk guy at Lenny's apartment to begin with? Why did he chase us? Who was the other guy that kicked the door down? Why did my cousin meet with us on Friday in the first place? Why did he tell me to contact this guy if we didn't see him again? I need to know, Andrew. You can go home if your ankle is feeling any better. I'll do this on my own if I have to."

"After nearly breaking my leg following you off a cliff? I'll stay right here, thank you."

"Your funeral."

"Yeah, probably."

The bathroom door swung open. Billy emerged with a

freshly shaven head, revealing the pale white scalp that had once held his long dark hair not even minutes earlier. For a second, Ray regretted not heeding his friend's words to abandon this place.

"That's been bothering me for a while," Billy said. "Finally time for a fresh start."

"Okay, weirdo." Andrew pointed to the radio. "Why do you want this thing so bad?"

"Because it's a doorway, stupid. This isn't for kids, you know. Lenny must have told you that much. You wouldn't understand any of this, and I can't even begin to explain it."

Ray waved Billy off. "It's my cousin that's missing, remember? I told you what I saw when I heard that creepy radio show the other night. I have to find him. I need to know the truth."

"He is okay."

"How do you know?" Ray bit the inside of his cheek. "After all this craziness I've been through, you can't expect me to believe that just by you saying it. Put yourself in my shoes. How would you react? Tell me where Lenny is, Spikes."

Billy stared blankly ahead for what felt like an eternity. It was impossible to tell if he was thinking of what to say or if he had forgotten where he even was. It didn't look like he'd thought about much in a long time, not with that empty glare on his face. Finally, after far too long, Billy opened his mouth and licked his lips.

"You've got a comfortable life, kid. This is a good town; I've seen it for the short time I've been here. You have family, friends, and a community that functions. Here is what you don't get, though. Most of that is gone outside of here. You haven't seen what we have —what we *know* is coming. Cherish what little time you've got left with those still here. Lenny's already left this world behind, and he isn't coming back. Come midnight, we'll all be in a better place. A place where we belong."

A dam broke in Ray's numb mind, and the heat rose in his gut. He bared his teeth at the bald punk. "Don't give us that! After everything I've seen, I deserve a real answer. Where are you planning on going? Why do you need the radio? Why did he leave in the first place?"

Billy rubbed the bridge of his nose and sighed. "I'm only going to say this once more. That particular radio is a doorway. Lenny used it to make preparations, and since he didn't come back, that means he's finished. The radio program tonight is the last broadcast. Those who listen will be taken away to the Real World, and they will never come back. If you go through, you can't return. That's it. There isn't anything else. I told you that you wouldn't get it."

"Then who were those guys at my cousin's apartment?"

"Those who only know half the story. As you've already experienced, the Y Signal doesn't take to everyone. Sometimes it . . . changes them. This is why Lenny didn't just parade it around like he was some kind of prophet with the elixir of life or some junk. The people showing up around town recently are those unworthy of the Y Signal, and they don't even know it. They're just trying to find the source, kinda like you. They are obsessed with something they can never own. That's why Lenny barely went out of his apartment. How else would you deal with that sort of thing?"

Andrew slapped his own forehead. "You all belong in the loony bin."

None of this made a difference. Ray still needed answers from the person who mattered the most here. Lenny had always been there for Ray, and that was reality. Whatever problems his cousin had, the boy would be there for him now and in whatever future waited ahead. That was what family was for. Leaving him with Yarbrough and that monster in some impossible alien space was not something Ray was willing to do.

"Well, I'm going with you," Ray said. "Andrew, stay here. I need to do this for Lenny."

"Be my guest," Billy replied. He tweaked the volume knob on the radio. "But I warned you."

"Plug your ears and don't look, Andrew." Ray knelt by his friend. "You don't want to go where this leads."

Andrew's lips creased hard against his teeth. "I don't get all this, and I really don't know why you won't let it go, at this point. We returned the radio, and we know your cousin is gone. He wanted to go, right? This has nothing to do with us. Just leave it there."

"I can't. Lenny wouldn't leave me."

Andrew sighed. "Didn't he just do that? You've always been a bit gullible. Families really aren't as simple as you think. One wrong turn and they will flip on you. But I already know what you're like when you make a decision. Either way, I'm not good for running right now, so I'll have to stay here. Don't get yourself killed."

"After today, I don't think anything could kill me."

Andrew forced himself up and into the bathroom. He plugged his ears and closed his eyes as he left the living room. "Just make it quick."

Billy fiddled with the knob and turned down the volume as the bathroom door closed. He paused before tuning it correctly. Lenny's friend and Ray leaned close when the bald punk finally flicked the power on.

"It's going to turn off automatically in a minute regardless," Billy called out to the closed bathroom. The bald punk leaned next to Ray. "No one is ever going to hear this again after it shuts itself down. Do you realize that? Last chance to turn back, kid."

"Ready when you are, Spikes."

"That man is dead. Whatever I am now will be revealed in seconds."

With those words, the radio's speakers screeched a sound-wave of static. The universe faded, and before Ray knew it he was no longer in the apartment, or even on Earth. He had left the old world behind. A gnawing feeling in his gut told him he would never return home again. The swirling fuzz of static cartwheeled through his brain.

This was the end of the line. There was no turning back now. The Y Signal waited. Within seconds he just knew that he would reach it, and everything would come into focus again. He had to keep the faith alive. No matter what it took, Ray would pierce this static and learn the truth.

Somewhere far away, the howl of a train whistle broke into the void, and it was getting closer. Ray felt his fists tighten beside his numb body. The last train was here.

Part Four
Last Train

It wasn't the same as the last time Ray listened to the radio. Whereas the previous trip into the ephemeral space forcefully warped the world and his mind into a fever dream of impossibilities, this journey was akin to the floor coming out from under him and plummeting into a moving crevice. Only black midnight surrounded him.

Ray dropped through the earth, kissing air in a flailing somersault, before landing directly on his face. The jarring sensation was over in an instant. Spikes of pain jabbed along his muscles with every attempt he made to lift himself back up.

Whispers in his ears faded to a harsh humidity that clung to his pores like bad summer weather. He wiped at his eyes, ignoring the sudden silence.

The shrill screech of a high-pitched whistle brought streaks of sweat down Ray's sore neck. Sound quickly returned to his world again as the clicking of large wheels rolling reverberated louder and louder in his numb mind. When he finally managed to stand, Ray quickly realized that clatter was coming in from the outside. Two walls comprised of glass windows on his left and right sheltered him from the source. A row of vacant blue seats lined up on either side of the thin aisle the boy had woken up in. Ray had been dropped into a train.

"*Who is this?*" Yarbrough said. His voice played overhead like a PA system. "*Children are not supposed to be here.*"

"*He's my cousin,*" Lenny replied. Ray's cousin's voice also echoed. "*Billy brought him.*"

Yarbrough growled. "*Throw him out before I do.*"

"*Calm down. You've been so on edge recently. It's almost over, so why are you getting so upset?*"

"*I will not be thrown off schedule. Not now. Deal with this, or I will.*"

The voices in Ray's ears then clicked off like a light switch, leaving him alone in the rolling train again. Not a single soul waited in the empty car. That voice was Lenny's—but where was he? That conversation told him they were somewhere on this train.

The boy stood up, his weight leaning on the ugly blue seat next to him. It took a moment to realize this was a real train, and his hand really was touching the interior of it.

The seats were lined up two by two on either side with an empty overhead luggage rack above. Large grey doors blocked the way into the next car before and behind him. Aside from the fact that nothing but a pitch red sky waited outside the windows, it looked just like any normal train would. This car wasn't too dissimilar to the one he had taken on a vacation back in the second grade. Ray massaged his sore arms as he scanned the car ahead. Where should he go?

"Lenny is going to be at the front," Billy said. The bald punk sat alone in one of the seats behind Ray, staring blankly ahead. "You better find him before we arrive at the station. Yarbrough didn't sound too happy to find you here."

"How is there a train here? There's never been a station in Burroughsvale."

"The Y Signal gave form to the gate we all must cross. Our minds need to be able to comprehend the journey or else we cannot accept it. Lenny helped set this one up, I'm sure. He's always been too accommodating to others. Once we reach the station, we will pick up the others and then depart to the real world."

A sudden sickness washed over Ray. The *real world*? What had Yarbrough done to these guys?

"There's something seriously off with you all," Ray said. "Why do you trust this Yarbrough so much? Is it because he wrote a bunch of weird and catchy songs? I've heard some of things he's been saying, you know. He's crazy—he should be locked up. He thinks he's some kind of psychic and can see the future. Did any of you think he might be lying about all this? No one can tell the future, Spikes. How can you not understand that the guy is off his rocker?"

A flicker of anger passed over Billy's face. He glanced out the window into the world of red, and the rage vanished into a relaxed grin. "It's you who doesn't understand anything. Kids are so dumb. I'd know, since I was one back when I had to grow up in that hell. This here is the end of the line. There's no future for you."

"Because a crazy musician told you."

"He *can* tell the future. You've heard the Y Signal, and so has Lenny. I'm sure your cousin has told you predictions that turned out to be true. Did you ever wonder where he got that information from?"

Doubt washed over Ray, not unlike that stupid radio had done to his soul the other night. He remembered some of the thoughts that had appeared in his head when he least expected them to. How did Lenny know about the movie the other night? He was so sure that *Judge Dredd* would be bad, too. Had Yarbrough really discovered a way of seeing the future?

But his uncertainty didn't stop on that notion. How did Yarbrough know he was *actually* being told the future? How did he know he wasn't being fooled or played with that crazy guy who burst into his apartment looking for Lenny? It could all be guesswork, parlor tricks, or inside information from some other source. Regardless, this was all too convenient. Why did Lenny believe it so easily? If Yarbrough really could see the future, then why were they running away instead of fixing things? There were too many questions Ray had, and no matter how much he thought on them he could not find an answer.

"I'll bring Lenny home on my own," Ray said.

"Do whatever you want." Billy yawned. "No one would ever want to go back after knowing the truth. I'll see you at the end of the line."

Ray charged towards the front of the car. The only reason he could tell he was moving forward was because of the signs inside the train. The outside showed nothing but a crimson glow of light with no wind or hint as to what the train even looked like—if it actually existed at all. The brightness outside increased the further the train barreled forward into the emptiness.

The boy dashed through car after car, seemingly in an endless loop of train. Each door effortlessly opened for him without much in the way of resistance. Instead, that same voice played over the invisible speakers just as it did back in the food court.

"*Deal with him,*" the crazed musician said. "*I've had enough distractions for one lifetime.*"

The voice fuzzed and bent overhead. Ray had to have been getting closer as it only cleared up as he ran through the train. Soon enough, a car door kicked open ahead of him, and a familiar face stepped through it to meet him in the center of the car. Lenny wore a black t-shirt and blue jeans with his hair neatly combed for the first time in ages. Much of the anxiousness in his face from Friday had dissipated. Despite his cleaner look, the dark circles under his eyes remained as they did before.

"What are you doing, Ray? You weren't supposed to use the radio; just give it to Billy."

"Then why did you tell me all that cryptic junk?"

"Because I needed you to make sure the radio didn't fall into the wrong hands, and Billy was too paranoid to leave his apartment. Anyone could have used it after I left, but no one else would have taken what I said seriously other than you. Everyone thinks I'm crazy. I don't blame them, though. This was the only way to keep this a secret from the outside world."

"Well, one of your friends was at your apartment today— the one we saw at the pizzeria. He got into a fight with some creep who kicked your door in."

"Brad? First the pizzeria and now this. Oh boy. He's been asking about the Y Signal for weeks, but I wouldn't tell him, and the night we met at the pizza place he was starting to lose it. He isn't fit for this. Not everyone is." His glare sharpened towards Ray. "Especially not kids."

"He's not the only weirdo. That other guy who showed up at your place while we were there was worse. He probably followed that Brad guy to the building. Is this why there are so many crazies hanging around town? You roll with quite a crowd, Lenny, but you don't belong here."

"I don't, huh?" Lenny laughed. "I'll bet your dad didn't even know I was missing, did he?"

Ray paused. It was true that his father just thought Lenny was being his usual aloof self, but he could hardly be blamed for that, especially considering where his cousin actually was at this very moment. No one made him do the weird things he did.

"He just thought you were being you. But this isn't you."

Lenny nodded mindlessly, his gaze darting across the car towards the endless haze of the outside world. He let out a hard breath before he scratched the back of his head. Ray's favorite cousin appeared to be trying to spout something stuck on the tip of his tongue.

"Billy was one of two people with that name when we ran in our group," Lenny said. "He had spiked hair, which is why we called him Spikes instead. Do you know what happened to the other

Billy? You remember the Strychnine Shooter guy in the news a few years back? No, you're too young. Some psycho went around pharmacies and drug stores injecting Strychnine into various medicines. Our friend unknowingly took some home with him inside his cold medicine. The Billy you met was the one who found our friend's lifeless body in the morning. He looked like he had crawled out of hell, his body contorted and pained, and not a single soul was there to help."

Ray's mouth dried. How was he supposed to reply to that? He'd never even seen a dead body outside of a packed funeral home. However, despite the story, it still didn't explain anything at all about this mess, and he was running out time. They could be at this so-called station at any moment.

"I'm sorry about your friend," Ray said. It did explain Billy's strange mood, but not why either of these guys would come here. "That has nothing to do with the Y Signal."

"It does. No one showed up to the funeral. Not his mom, not his brothers, not any of the other guys. It was just me, Brad, and the ex-punk who followed you here through the radio. That was about five years ago, not long after they picked up John Gotti. Remember him? That one was all over the media. Old Billy wasn't important enough for the news—he was insignificant. You've never been to the city, Ray. You don't know what it's like. They can clean and polish the stone and concrete all they want, and they can throw as many dirtbags in cells as they want, but it's never going to be anything but a trash pile where people sink deep inside and are never seen again. My friend is dead, and no one even noticed; no one will ever notice, and soon enough all trace of him will be gone forever. I can't just go on with a happy grin like some lobotomy patient. That's not living a life; accepting their reality is giving up and embracing evil as normality: as if it's supposed to be this way. I may be many things, but I will not accept a lie as truth."

Ray took a moment to process what his favorite cousin had just said. It was rambling and nearly incoherent, but there was a passion hidden in there. His friend died, and that meant the world is fake? No, it didn't connect at all. Ray might have just been a kid, but he knew cowardice when he saw it.

"You're running away!" the boy shouted. "Instead of trying to work through this, you just decide to split and leave us all behind.

What happened to you, Lenny?"

"I'm not running from anything." Ray's cousin jabbed a thumb backwards at the car doors behind him. "I don't have anything to run away from. My parents split long ago; the bands I cared about are gone, and there is nothing left on the road ahead. Yarbrough might be rough around the edges, but you know he's right."

"He isn't. Nothing you've told me proves he isn't anything other than a . . . what's it called? A Charlatan! Come back to Burroughsvale. It's definitely better than this place. Forget that dangerous creep, and let's go home."

"We're not hurting anyone with what we're doing, Ray. Just go out the exit, and you'll return back home. It's a long drop, and a bit scary the first time, but you'll wake up fine. I promise. You have people to go back to. Enjoy the time you have left before you're me. You kids deserve it."

"Don't trust that guy!" Ray bared his teeth. "I remember that broadcast. Did you not notice the weird ape man or the gross plants all over? There was this giant bird-thing outside the window. You just accept that? That is far less normal than anything that goes on back home. He's hiding something from all of you, and you don't want to face it. You guys aren't being told the whole truth."

Lenny grimaced and shook his head. "That's the Lost Race. Yarbrough discovered them when he first explored the signal. They were banished there in the True World long ago. That's what our parents never told us. Or at least our parents' parents, however far that goes back. It's all lies regardless. Those *weird apes* are helping him achieve his goal. We have a lot of lies to undo."

"You don't know that's true, Lenny! They could be using him to get you all lined up for a snack or maybe even as slaves in that dark world. It could be anything. Use your head! Why aren't you thinking through this at all?"

"You misunderstand me, Ray. I don't care. None of us care. Whatever we meet over there will be better than here, even if it kills us."

"Stop talking like that, you idiot. Did you forget we're family? Maybe *I* want you around. Some part of you refused to tell me about the Y Signal because you *know* it's not right. You might say differently, but I know you. You're the one lying. You're doing it to yourself."

"Stop babbling," Lenny said. He glanced away from his cousin. "You'll forget about me when I go, just like your dad already has. Maybe not soon, but someday. I'm pretty irrelevant in the grand scheme of things. Most of us are. It's best you experience it now rather than later. Loss builds character." Lenny chuckled to himself. "Now I sound like my dad."

Ray seized his cousin's wrist. "I don't care what you want. Come on, we're going home."

The boy took a few steps towards the side exit with his cousin in tow when a harsh burst of static nearly deafened him. The entire train rocked as if an earthquake had rattled the car. Ray and Lenny each tumbled over sideways into the seats. The train seemed to spin like it was attempting an aileron roll, as impossible as that was. Reality spun around. Ray rolled about until he hit the floor on all fours and felt his breakfast against his teeth.

When the train finally stopped shaking, a familiar lean man wearing a green sweater and slacks entered the car. Yarbrough's face was so red it looked as if it might melt off at any second.

"Throw the stupid git out already!"

Lenny struggled to sit up from his prone position in the seat. He gagged on a breath. "I was about to before you stormed in here. Stop freaking out. I have no intention of letting kids come with us."

"This arrogant little puke thinks he has it all figured out, butting into our business with his stupid, uneducated views he cobbled together in the sandbox." Yarbrough stomped towards Ray. "I walked Fear City in the '80s. I saw the fall of the Berlin Wall, and I was in town when Kurt *supposedly* killed himself. What's this brat seen but bad Hollywood movies that numb the mind into accepting decay? I've seen the future. There is nothing ahead but death. At least, this runt will be allowed to live in ignorance until the end comes."

Ray forced himself to stand up. His gut continued its acrobat act as he steadied himself before the musician. "Just because you got some predictions right doesn't mean you got them all. You said it yourself the first time I went under: there are many futures. They can't all be as bad as you believe."

"And yet, this is the world we live in, brat. I know all my predictions will come true because I've seen them already happen on a smaller scale, over and over. It's human nature to do the wrong thing and drag everyone else into the resulting mess. This is the one eternal truth of our whole evil existence. We are simply leaving the rest to their own devices while we seek a better future in the Real World. They'll all die, and they'll all deserve it."

Lenny looked at Yarbrough sideways, but Ray didn't back down. Instead, he shoved the former rock star with all the anger he could muster. "You don't get to decide that. Just because you lucked out and found this Y Signal doesn't make you God."

Yarbrough pushed the boy back with an unexpected zeal, sending Ray to the floor. "Piss off, you know-nothing runt. I summoned the Y Signal myself through blood and sacrifice. That red view you are seeing outside is a result of all my effort to save us. To slip inside reality itself: that's the power I earned. Anyone else could have found it, any of our parents, our ancestors, our leaders, but none of them did. Not only did they fail to harness this force, they sealed the world off, and left us alone in the dark with nothing but noise and plastic. They deserve the genocide they will cause to themselves, and my only regret is that I won't be there to laugh at them in the face about it as they suffer."

"Yarbrough," Lenny said. He lowered his voice. "This kid isn't that big of a deal. Let it go. We came here because we didn't want a part in the old world anymore, not because we want to destroy it or see people die."

"I'm not planning on destroying anything. I'm letting it die. I can see possibilities, hundreds of thousands of routes we can take to reach the future—this is the gift of the Y Signal. Using logic, pattern recognition, deduction, and probability—things they don't teach kindergartners like this brat—I can easily surmise the fate of the brainless sleepwalkers that inhabit the 20th century. I see a pit ahead, followed by an implosion like you've never seen before. And that's the truth. What prediction would you like next? A terrorist shooting in Israel or a bombing in Sri Lanka? I don't even need the Y Signal for something like that."

Lenny rubbed at his clearly tired eyes. "You told me that leaving would be like we never existed. We would step out of existence. One of those other futures you mentioned as a possibility might occur instead. Us taking off would be better for everyone."

"Who cares?" Yarbrough replied, saliva splashing from his lips. "A lot of people are going to get what is coming to them. That's all I care about. Now, enough of this. The platform is waiting for us, as are our new friends. Throw this little punk off the train, and let's go."

The boy's anger flared, and his voice rose despite himself. Ray jumped back up again. "I'm not going anywhere!"

He charged into Yarbrough with a sudden burst of adrenaline and knocked the jerk over. The two rolled backwards as the train rattled with their tossed bodies. The entire structure flipped was as if the car itself had been tackled. The whole train flopped around in an impossible barrel roll with Yarbrough, Ray, and Lenny, striving to maintain their balance as they were thrown about, banging against the interior. Metal screeched inside the twisting space.

The boy and his enemy grabbed at each other. It didn't matter that Yarbrough clearly had the strength and size advantage when he had been so thrown off balance. The train spun, sending the parties all over the inside of the car. Windows crunched as bodies slammed into them. The grappling pair landed against the door at the end of the car and Lenny dropped into the seats again. The train regained its proper balance at the same moment Yarbrough did.

"Get off my train!" The ex-rocker seized Ray's collar and punched him square in the stomach. Ray gagged as Yarbrough kicked his doubled-over body. He sneered at the boy hitting the ground again. "You have no place in my world."

The boy gasped for air as Yarbrough threw open the side exit. No wind flooded inside, only dead silence. Ray gripped the nearby seat as his breath struggled in his chest. Humidity smacked his face from the rouge void outside where no ground existed—just endless red skies. Only harsh scarlet light existed inside this foreign space—and whatever lay below.

Spittle splashed through Yarbrough's pointed teeth as he dragged his victim forward. "Go home and fix your own damned world!"

"*It's your world, too,*" Ray said. He coughed, his breaths pumped jaggedly from his sore chest. "You can't just walk away. What about your family, your band, and your fans?"

"They have chosen their fate. You are all getting what you have coming to you."

"Forget it, Yarbrough," Lenny said. He put a hand on the ex-rock star's shoulder. "You've done enough here today. It's time to go home."

Lenny shoved Yarbrough out the door to the train. The madman's clasping fingers lost its grip on Ray's shirt as he plummeted down into the crimson horizon. Ray fell against the side of the door, holding tightly as he watched his enemy drop. The former rock star fell out of sight and soon even his shouts disappeared into the bottomless infinity underneath the train.

Lenny pulled the flailing Ray back into the train. He steadied the boy, keeping an eye on the endless pit of a world underneath the vehicle. "You have to go home, too."

"Why did you push him out? Won't he just come back?"

"It's already past midnight back home. Time converges here at the time the Y Signal was sent out, and Yarbrough's radio is the source of it. You and Billy sent it out when you came here. No one else can come through now until it is turned on again. Yarbrough won't be able to come back because it is already after the broadcast time back on Earth. It's too late. The train has left the station, and there's no turning back. It's time for you to leave, too. You don't belong here, Ray. That's the only thing I'm certain of anymore."

"He was manipulating you the entire time, Lenny. You know that now, right? He just wanted to set up shop in some new world as a king or whatever. He didn't want to help anybody."

Lenny smiled weakly. "I knew he was on edge, but I thought he was getting over it. His obsession never quite died out, but it apparently just got worse the longer he was in the Y Signal. Maybe nobody really has resistance to it like I thought they might. He became better at hiding his slipping grip, until you showed up. That's why I didn't just tell anyone about the Y Signal. At first, I thought I'd just take a bunch of people like me to this new place like it was an adventure. You know, give them a second chance at life in a better place where they could find themselves. Sorta like moving to a new country or town, I guess. But after seeing Yarbrough snapping like he did, I'm not so sure of that anymore. People like him need to stay among the living. Otherwise, they slide deeper into their own ego."

"You don't belong here, either, Lenny."

"I can't just abandon those people on the platform, Ray. The whole reason they're here is because they think the world has already left them behind. They've given up, just like I had. I need to take the train to the station and tell them what happened with

Yarbrough. I brought them to this place, so it's my problem. We aren't that far from the station, either. I should get ready."

"I'll go with you."

Lenny shook his head. "I don't know if I can even stop this train without Yarbrough. At least, you can go home. Live your life. Enjoy your summer as best you can. You won't get a lot of them in your life, regardless of whatever happens next. Don't worry about me anymore, either. I have to make up for what I did. I'm not running away again."

"What did I come here for, then?" Ray felt the anger boil in his sore gut. "Do you have any idea what I've been through since Friday? Now you're just telling me to walk away?"

"Relax!" Lenny laughed and smacked Ray on the back. "There are people I have to see, and things to think about. Go home and tell your dad that I'll be over to shoot pool with him again soon."

"Please, stop this."

Lenny grinned. "If it's any consolation, the next Superman movie should be out in the next two years. It'll be worth it. Trust me."

"What do you—"

Before Ray could finish, Lenny shoved the boy out of the open door. Ray's cousin waved to him as the scarlet fog enveloped the passing train whole. He dropped like a concrete block into the bay of emptiness. Nothing in the void remained aside from his own flailing body spinning into the depths of this impossible space. He thought he was shouting, but eventually lost his voice in the choking silence. The red vortex closed above Ray at the same moment that the world turned white. All his senses cut out and died.

And then it was all gone. The world had disappeared just as suddenly as it first arrived.

The apartment popped back into existence like it just remembered to be there. Reality returned as the train became nothing but a memory. He coughed on the stale air.

Ray hit the solid floor, face first. His legs trembled like he'd been left out in a blizzard. He rubbed at his sore jaw, and slowly sat back up. Everything inside of him hurt. The cheap carpet felt oddly soothing under his torn-up palms.

When the realization that he was alive hit him, Ray sprang to his feet. "Lenny?!"

But his cousin didn't answer.

Moonlight slipped through the blinds of Billy's apartment and bathed the place in a harsh blue glow. There was no clock to be seen on the wall, but he knew the time. Lenny had already told him, and he always told the truth. Midnight had long since departed this place. The broadcast was over.

"Anyone here?" he called out. "Am I awake?"

"*Not for much longer.*"

Behind the couch emerged the limping body of Yarbrough. He clutched his right eye as if it had been punched in, and his breaths pumped hard. Before Ray could say anything, Yarbrough kicked the boy with his twitching left leg, knocking him down to the floor.

Ray scampered backwards across the carpet on his elbows. "What are you doing here?"

"This is *my* radio, you git. I entered through it, same as you did. Where else did you think I'd fall when your stupid cousin pushed me out of my Y Signal? Now I have to work from nothing because of you and your wretched kin. This is why I hate kids and weaklings. Oh well, at least I'll get to break your spine."

"Just calm down," Ray said. Through the dark of the apartment behind Yarbrough, a moving shadow slipped in through the moonlight beams of the night. Was it Lenny? The boy decided to keep talking. "You can make it so that those things you saw never happened. This is your second chance!"

"I don't know by heart which of those events will occur and which won't. Whatever the Y Signal was, whatever source lent me the power to see into the future, much of it was like putting pieces together of events already happening that lead to obvious conclusions. But sometimes, they don't always happen *quite* that way. It was more like it was showing me very educated guesses that only the most aware of us could puzzle out. Sort of like obvious conclusions to the path the world has decided to take. There are many futures, in a sense."

"Wait! That's it! You just said it yourself. You don't actually know. Now that you're here you can change what you do know. You don't have to run away anymore."

"There is nothing to run from, and nothing to save. Nothing has changed with your meddling. It's all going to burn, starting with you."

Yarbrough took a step towards the fallen Ray, his toothy smile dancing with joy in the harsh moonlight. Nothing would ever stop this crazed loon's mad quest to reshape reality. He had long since left this world behind. Yarbrough took one look over towards the window and stopped.

"Wait," the madman said. "Where is my radio?"

Out of the dark behind Yarbrough, moved a smaller figure. Andrew had a black bulky object between has hands as he jumped off the couch towards the psycho. Ray's friend brought the radio down on top of Yarbrough's head with a hard swing. The old equipment broke, sprinkling pieces of metal, plastic, and wires, across the floor. Yarbrough grunted and leaned over, clutching the back of his bleeding skull.

But something else burst from the broken device, and it wasn't a radio signal. Streams of red liquid ejected out of the shattered parts and twisted wires, almost like veins full of blood. It doused Yarbrough from head to toe like a water bucket. Heavy steam burned against his skin and wrapped around his limbs, chest, and throat. He screamed as the shattered radio appeared to grab at him.

"What is this?" Yarbrough shouted. "What did you do?"

The blood water clung to Yarbrough like a thousand tiny leaches growing into snakes. The mass stretched down to the carpet like living goo and attached against the carpet. It spread under his feet not unlike a living puddle. After widening to the circumference of Yarbrough's twisting body, the gunk pulled him into the floor like quicksand. It was eating him?

"*You destroyed the future*," Yarbrough said, his voice croaking. He dropped down into the red tar, as if the ground decided to disappear. "*You deserve everything you're going to get.*"

With those last words, Yarbrough plummeted into the red haze. As soon as he vanished from sight, the blood liquid solidified and hardened on top of the carpet. The crust of crimson evaporated into thin air, taking even the radio remains with it as if they too were liquid. All that remained of Yarbrough's Y Signal had just completely disappeared like a bad dream in the morning light. Not a scrap remained.

Ray and Andrew stared at the bare carpet for a long time before either of them spoke again. Whatever the Y Signal had been, it definitely was no friend. Whether Yarbrough understood that or not at the end was anyone's guess. All Ray could think was how thankful he was that he didn't drop the radio when he was climbing down the balconies earlier. Imagining himself in Yarbrough's place sent a chill down his back into his trembling legs. He definitely didn't want to think about that now. Slowly, he found the willpower to stand back up.

"My parents are going to ground me so bad," Andrew said. He kept staring at the bare carpet. "I fell asleep in the backroom with my foot elevated on the bed. It feels a lot better now. I didn't think you'd be gone that long. It's past midnight, you know."

Ray blinked. "Is that all you can think about right now?"

"I . . . no. I'd rather pretend nothing happened. Don't even want to think about it."

There were many things Ray wanted to say, but they all felt rather unimportant in the grand scheme of things, especially considering what had just happened. All traces or information about the Y Signal had just been obliterated and erased from his life in a single moment. It might as well have never happened.

"We should get out of here," Ray said. "Our parents really will kill us for staying out so late."

The two boys made for the door, Andrew still unsteady on his feet. They closed the bare apartment behind them and took to their bikes outside. There wasn't a single soul left on the playground, just as Ray figured there wouldn't be so late at night. Even during summer vacation, kids needed to sleep, and so did the town. Being able to go home after playing is what made playing worthwhile in the first place. He now believed that simple truth more than ever.

They rode their bikes across the empty streets of Burroughsvale, encountering little in the way of passing cars. Perhaps Lenny was right and their earlier pursuers had already departed through their own radios into the Y Signal. Unlike Yarbrough or Ray, they didn't appear to return at midnight, so did that mean they were trapped in that impossible red space? Did Lenny fail at his task, or did something else happen to him inside the signal? Ray just had to trust in his cousin's words that he would handle it.

As Andrew and Ray flew down the barren streets of Burroughsvale, the quiet did little to ease the tension. Instead, they talked in stilted tones about what they would be doing next week. There was plenty of summer left, after all. But still Ray couldn't forget what had just happened, and he doubted he ever would.

Lenny had never given his cousin a reason to doubt him before. Even if he finally realized Yarbrough was full of it by the end and told Ray to live regardless of whatever future awaited him, his older cousin shouldn't have been in that position in the first place. Ray would never understand that generation. Things were not that bad, and they always had the chance of getting better. The Y Signal was now gone, and the future was open again. They could once more look forward to whatever lay ahead. People weren't perfect, but they always had the chance to set it right again. His cousin proved that to him at the end.

Until Lenny came back, Ray would keep being a kid. He would have to enjoy as much of whatever life threw his way as he could. Then the boy would show his cousin how wrong he was to run away. It would be different next time. There are no real last trains— there is always another one in the morning.

A thousand Julys from now, summer would still be around, long after they were all gone from this Earth. Why waste throwing it all away on what *might* happen in the meantime? For now, he had many bright days ahead to look forward to, and he would do so with open arms. Summer meant promise, and it was promise he would fulfill.

Ray pedaled madly ahead into the night.

"Slow down, Ray," Andrew called after him. "You want to get killed?"

"No way, man. I've got places to be!"

And he would make sure that he always did. That is, after all, what summer is all about.

Rusted Autumn Skies

The warm winds blew away with the oncoming night. The days grew shorter, and the cold came in like a lion. The leaves leaped from the trees, and the colors deepened and darkened. Your mother made you wear thicker clothing with longer sleeves, and your father lamented the sun setting earlier. You knew it was over now. T-shirt weather gives way to sweaters!

Chipper parents dragged their somber children to the store to buy notebooks and schoolbags. Even if you didn't have to worry about the inevitable return of school until September (though the school board did consider pushing the start date earlier!), somehow August still hung over you like a dark cloud, even as you aged. There was no escaping the end.

Beaches cleared, theaters quieted, and grandparents silently frowned as they prepared to lose their grandchildren until Christmas when there are yet more uncomfortable sweaters to give out. Another year notched off the belt.

But as time passed, you realized the comfort hiding in the changing winds—the promise of an open future. The memories fade, but the experiences embedded in your very marrow gives comfort. Because, even though you get it wrong more than you'd like, you look forward to the next summer. It's another chance. Eventually, the warm winds will blow the cold out, and the Endless Summer will return. Though the years roll on, the muscle memory of the old days remains forever.

Summer always returns.

You close your eyes and remember. You can see it growing closer and closer, brighter and bigger and louder than it ever was before, like a carnival it clatters into your tired thoughts to overtake the weariness of the *day in day out* of the passing years.

Then one day you wake up to see it one last time. That is when it hits you like a freight train: endless really does mean forever and ever. It truly does go on. No more sweaters, no more cold, just a warm summer sun stretching on forever.

Memories fade, and you wake. It's time to get up and face the chill. Hopefully, you remembered that sweater!

A long winter awaits.

SNOW OUT

Part One
A-Bomb for H Street

The howling wind slashed through his headache like a Ginsu blade from one of those commercials, leaving Ray huddled in his mass of covers as a rabbit would hide in its hole from a fox. He fought this burgeoning static inside his mind with those familiar opening chords to "Champagne Supernova," the last song from the recent Oasis album, and one that stuck with him since he first heard that CD. It allowed him to focus on an escape, something outside of the lingering memories of the past summer that kept forcing its way in. 1995 was not what it was cracked up to be.

He tossed and turned in the guest bed as the memories forced themselves into his brain again. The moment the sweat pooled on his neck, he shot up. Ray ran his palms across his skin, almost wishing he could take another shower. It was too late now, though.

The darkness in the small bedroom was made worse by the screaming breeze outside the heavily curtained window. He tried to turn the light on, but it was still a no-go. The power was already out when he went to bed early after dinner, and it seemingly had not returned. He quickly changed into the same mustard yellow sweater and navy blue pants he wore yesterday.

The boy felt around in the dark of the hallway. The rest of the apartment remained black as night, not even the Christmas tree by the kitchen shone a single light. If the couple of candles around the coffee table hadn't been left burning, he would definitely not have been able to see three inches in front of his face. It was like he had woken up in the grave.

A wind knocked up against the wall the exact moment a voice spoke out. "Lenny?"

The mumbling of Ray's grandmother caused him to jump just a little. He shook off the frazzled nerves and turned towards her.

"No, Granny, it's me," Ray said. His hoarse voice almost made him sound like he was doing a bad impression of himself. Ray cleared his throat before he spoke again. "Lenny is still . . . *out*."

"Oh."

Ray's grandmother shifted in her position on the couch, the heavy patchwork blanket sliding over her ruffled white hair as she lay back down. Without her glasses on, she always looked tired, though she always looked tired these days regardless.

"You don't have to sleep on the couch, Granny, I keep telling you that. If you're going to stay in Lenny's apartment then you can sleep in his room."

"That wouldn't be right," she mumbled. "Every boy needs their own bed, especially my grandson. I can't ask him to sleep on his own couch. Shoot, I left the candles burning."

There was no way for her to know that Lenny hadn't just wandered off like a cowboy in those old midnight movies they all used to watch together. He wasn't even on planet Earth, as far as Ray knew. Regardless, he couldn't explain that to her.

"You worry too much, Granny. He'll be back home before you know it."

Ray didn't like to lie, but he didn't know how else to reassure her. Lenny told him he would return back during the summer, but he never did. How could Ray tell his own grandmother that her grandson fell victim to a demented occultist rock singer who tried to rip them out of reality itself? She'd consider him as crazy as Ray already did.

What even was reality anymore?

The events of the summer had only really happened to a small number of the residents of Burroughsvale. Aside from Ray and his best friend Andrew, only Ray's grandmother thought something was off about the fact that her other grandson never came home again. Everyone else simply thought he was being a black sheep. Isn't that what weirdos do? Don't they just go off because the wind tells them to? That's what Ray's dad always said. Life is wherever the wind takes you.

But Lenny had given that up because he'd seen the future, or so he thought. If he'd truly seen it all, then did he foresee this storm happening, too?

"The power's still out?" she asked. She checked her watch, shook it, then grimaced at the old thing. "What time is it?"

"The clock on the wall still says midnight, but its not moving. None of them are. Something's up with the weather."

"I swear, the Second Coming's got to be on the way. First

the barrage of out-of-towners during the summer, then the mass arrests in fall—I still can't believe they found those two men fighting in Lenny's apartment—and now those people collapsing into comas. Madness!"

"Granny, I need some fresh air. My head still hurts. Will Mom and Dad will be back soon?"

"They've still got your brother at that retreat for advanced children. They said they'd be home by Christmas. They still have a few days left, so don't worry. Sleep didn't help the headache, Ray?"

"No." He scratched the back of his skull. A low hum echoed in the depths of his brain like feedback from an amplifier. "I just need to walk around a bit. Granny?"

She slumped back down into the couch, a low snore rumbling out of her throat. How tired was she? Ray decided to leave her to it. Plenty of people around here seemed overly tired these days. He approached the window, wincing with every step.

Endless squall blocked any visibility of the real world waiting outside his cousin's old apartment. The impression of a vice squeezing his head continued unabated as he scanned the emptiness filled with screeching white wind. The dead space could have been mistaken for ground zero of some kind of bombing.

But that was ridiculous. Nothing like that could ever happen in Burroughsvale. The world couldn't just end overnight. All he needed was some fresh air, then this would all clear up.

Ray put on his winter clothes that he left in the closet. He sat on the living room chair and slid his boots on. The boy threw on his jacket, gloves, and winter hat, before taking another deep breath. Maybe it really was the end of the world. He shook the thought off, put out the candles, and left the apartment, locking the door behind him.

"You promised you'd come back, Lenny. Where did you go?"

Everything would be fine in the morning. He just needed some air.

***

Andrew stared up at the crucifix above the altar, his knees trembling under the pain that blazed in his mind's eye. Eyes watering, he wondered if the guys next to him on the pew would think he was crying, but they were apparently lost in their own little world. It was late, after all.

Danny had his arms folded and foot tapping. He scratched his blond hair and spun his cap between his fingers. He clearly hadn't been used to being up this early—or late. It was quite impossible to know what time it actually was recently. Danny pulled up the collar on his winter coat and sighed.

"I thought we'd be doing more interesting stuff for a sleepover, guys. This Christmas has already been a bust so far. Now we're sitting in a church."

George shrugged. "It isn't like we're always going to get to do things like this, you know."

"What does that mean?" Danny asked.

"It means what it means."

"Could you two kindly shut up?" Andrew said. He bit his lip as a wave of pain rolled over his eyes. "We'll go in a second. I just need a moment."

There was a short pause before George broke the silence. "Why didn't you want me to invite Ray to stay over? Ever since we started sixth grade you two have been acting odd."

"Naw," Danny said. "Since summer. You two are morons. Just make up already."

The compulsion Andrew had to throttle the two of them subsided when he thought about his old friend. There was nothing he could say as to why Ray wasn't with them except that ever since summer had ended, whenever the two of them saw each other, awkward memories returned. Perhaps a part of Andrew wanted to forget the thing that came out of that radio. Maybe if he didn't see Ray, he wouldn't be reminded of the sight of Yarbrough, the guitarist for the Panorama Agents, being dragged into some hell space through the very floor. Ray's presence always brought those memories back.

The truth, however, was not quite so dramatic. Since the school year started, Andrew had been seeing more and more strange sights, in his dreams and waking life. Pictures of places he had never seen before. Memories of these visions allowed bursts of static to fill his ears—the same static from when he broke that radio.

But Yarbrough was gone. He never returned from being attacked by that *thing*. Neither did the strangers that had been seen around town. Well, aside from the few that had either been arrested or fled of their own accord when fall arrived. Today, no trace remained of them in Burroughsvale. It was as if the Y Signal had never existed.

So why was this static bursting into his brain now? It had been getting worse since the school year started, preventing him from enjoying his last year in Elementary. Would this stick with him for the rest of his life? Maybe if it didn't kill him first.

Andrew pushed the thought from his mind, finishing up his prayers. At least, he could get some relief in the quiet of this church. Eventually, the static faded away.

"Father Vic will let us out," he said, standing up. "Don't worry, I'm good now."

Danny rolled his eyes. "Finally. We can get some early morning gaming in before George's 'rents get up. Hey, wanna see if Ultratech is open yet? They might have *Donkey Kong Country 2* in. I doubt anyone else is up right now to grab it first."

"I don't even know what time it is," Andrew said. He checked the watch his dad gave him before leaving on that marriage counseling vacation with his mom. It had stopped, just like every other clock around here had. "This snowstorm must have done something weird to electronics."

"What?" George slapped his winter cap back on his big head. "Clocks run on batteries, man. Must be something worse going on than a little snow."

Andrew feigned a smile. "Of course the boy scout would know."

"Oh shut up, you guys." Danny had already gotten halfway up the aisle by the time the other two were dressed. "It's nothing but a winter storm. Let's get back to George's place and out of this cold. Don't make me knock your heads together."

Andrew put it all out of his head. There couldn't be anything else going on in Burroughsvale. The Y Signal had been destroyed; Yarbrough was gone, and nothing crazy had happened since the summer ended. He would just have to deal with his headaches and see if his parents would get him a doctor's appointment, whenever they got back. Hopefully before Christmas got here.

Though his folks had been having a tough time, they'd

gotten better since their summer retreat. Unfortunately, he hadn't, though it wasn't as if he could tell them why. Would his Baby Boomer parents really understand that their Generation Y son had seen a strange light in between the fabric of reality itself that still tickled at his brain half a year later? They didn't believe in this sort of thing as it was.

Andrew mumbled his goodbye to Father Vic and shuffled forward mindlessly out of the church. Cold wind kicked him in the face as the door closed behind him. White squall coated the night, at least, he *thought* it was night. Christmas lights floating like fireflies in a fogged swamp were all that punctured the dark. Endless snow pushed against him with every stepped he made through the tall white banks.

"We need to get back before my folks get up," George said, his voice caught on the wind.

Danny spat some snow from his mouth. "Can you even see the street signs?"

Their voices faded in and out as Andrew walked on, the inexplicable static momentarily breaking through the wind and howling into his thoughts. He winced, rubbing his temples. The guys were going on mentioning something about Christmas, but he wasn't listening.

He had watched Yarbrough die, hadn't he? That psycho was dragged through reality itself after Andrew hit him with his own radio. The pit in his stomach growled as he thought on it. What if he wasn't dead at all? There was no body. But if he wasn't dead, then was he responsible for these strange headaches? Did he have something to do with the random people collapsing all over town? According to Ray, Yarbrough wanted to take his chosen people to a new world, whatever that meant. Maybe this was his revenge for being stopped. Maybe this was the end of the world.

"Andrew!" George yelled in his ear. "Where are you going? Stop!"

Andrew paused. He looked up to find he was standing in the Elementary School parking lot. When did he get here? He rubbed his sore skull.

Danny grabbed his shoulder. "What's up? We kept calling but you wouldn't stop."

"I'm fine." Andrew wrenched his shoulder free. "This weather is doing a number on me."

"Good for you," Danny said. "You just took us like a block or two away from George's house. Wait a second. What's that?"

The three glanced around the school and stared into the field behind the building. It had once been home to a small woods that had been cleared out months ago to make way for yet another apartment complex. Soon enough, all the trees between here and the river would be gone forever. But that wasn't what he cared about at that moment.

Instead, he focused on the lone structure that could be seen through the snowstorm. In the middle of the wide open field was a building, a three story place made of old brick that was as cracked as the old windows it housed. Hard yellow light shone out into the squall, somehow piercing the veil of the storm just as easily as the distant Christmas lights did.

But there was never a building before—he had even passed by here yesterday on the way to George's house. Where did it come from? The static in his head built as he scanned it over.

An abnormal metal mass on top of the building blew awkwardly in the wind. It was difficult to make out in the haze, but now he knew what it was. He recognized this place as a radio station.

And he had been led here.

"This is impossible," George muttered.

Andrew bit his lip and swore. He charged towards the field, scampering over the fence blocking him from his goal. It was Yarbrough! It had to be. His friends soon joined him, and they all pushed through the snowstorm.

A different sort of cold blew into Andrew's bones as he took giant steps through the deep snow. Ice frosted his blood, but it didn't cool his resolve. The static in his mind told him one thing.

The Y Signal was here.

***

The winter wind whispered in Ray's ears as he descended H Street. It sounded something like Andrew's voice, but the two of them hadn't talked in ages. It could have just been guilt nipping at him again. It was Ray's fault that Andrew got involved in this Y Signal business to begin with. It was no wonder he had been acting distant. That disaster with Yarbrough and Lenny was his own problem, anyway. He would be better to face solve that issue alone.

Chills slipped through his winter coat, even as he hugged his chest tight. Sure it was December, but why was it this cold out? Only those ever-present Christmas lights reminded him that he was still on Earth and not in some forgotten hell-void. A dab of red pain splashed just behind his eye sockets. The buzzing in his brain was getting worse, and he didn't know how to stop it.

Ray charged into the convenience store, thankfully still open. The lights were oddly low, but he didn't care. The acoustic sounds of "Wonderwall" by Oasis brought him back down to Earth. He was able to focus on the row of junk food before him more easily.

"Aren't you a bit young to be out this late?"

He looked up to the teenage girl behind the counter. She had her blonde hair back in ponytail and wore a plain blue sweater and battered blue jeans which matched her eyes. It seemed clear that she went to high school. Maybe in tenth grade? She folded her arms and jutted her chin at him.

"Hey," she said. "Do you got the time?"

"No. The clocks are acting screwy."

"Here, too. My dumb little sister was all kinds of paranoid so she insisted she come to work with me. Kids are stupid. I don't even know how long I'm on this shift for."

"Must be some sort of power problem." He winced at a flare of pain. A trickle of sweat dripped into his eye. "Do you have any Jolt Cola? I need something with a kick."

She sighed. "Fresh out."

He rubbed at his head. Without warning, the static burst in his skull like a popped balloon in his head. He held back a scream as he stumbled backwards.

"What's wrong, kid?"

"It's the Y Signal," he heard himself say.

A pause followed. "What did you say?"

The lights browned. Ray caught his balance before they flickered back on. When they lit up once more, the static vanished. He sighed his relief, ignoring the cashier as she repeated her question.

He shook his head at her. "Nothing, I'm just sleepy."

"Hey, I know him," another girl said. "Ray? What are you doing here?"

Ray squinted towards the counter where it looked like the

cashier sprang a midget clone of herself, though he knew that wasn't the case. Kristin Oliver held a yawn at bay with one hand as she leaned over the magazine rack towards him. He knew her from his class.

"Me?" he replied. "I live down the street. What are you doing?"

The older girl laughed. "She's a nosy brat."

"Shut up, Becky," Kristin said. She elbowed her taller sister. "Don't you have to do stock?"

"Yeah, whatever."

The cashier disappeared into the backroom while the two of them talked. Ray breathed a bit easier with her gone. Kristin was a little less abrasive, but not by much.

"You work here?" he asked. "Aren't you a bit young?"

"Becky is my sister, genius. Why shouldn't I be here with her?"

"Most kids stay at home, moron. They don't usually go to work with their older siblings. Aren't your parents worried?"

"No," she said. Kristin bit her lip and glanced at the storeroom behind the counter before she spoke again. "My dad collapsed a few days back. He's in the hospital, and my mom is there with him. People around town keep passing out, some into comas. It's weird. I wish I knew what was going on."

"Who knows? It's been a weird year. I'll be glad when it's gone."

"Is this what you said?" the cashier asked. Becky came out of the back room holding a CD jewel case. She presented it to Ray. The familiar cover of a barren midnight parking lot lit by a lone lamppost stared back at him. "The last album by the Panorama Agents, right? *Y Signal.*"

Now it was Kristin's turn to sigh like her older sister. "What do dead rock bands have to do with anything, Becky?"

"They're not dead, their guitarist just up and disappeared. They plan on doing more without him. Not that you'd get it. Don't you still listen to Janet Jackson albums?"

Ray knew all too well what the older girl meant. He stared at that familiar iconic cover with the nearly transparent album title. The opening feedback burst of "Sidewalk Philosophy" slashed into his mind before the rolling toms brought the headache back. Tears formed in his eyes as he attempted to shake the feeling off. It took a moment for him to realize he wasn't imagining it—the song was actually playing on the stereo system around them.

Or was it? Neither girl appeared to notice anything as they went on like nothing had changed.

"The Y Signal," Becky said. "I used to listen to the broadcast all the time until it suddenly stopped last summer. But now that I think about it, this weirdness with random people passing out happened not long after the show stopped broadcast, didn't it? It's only gotten worse since winter started. Does Yarbrough have something to do with this?"

The twinkle in her eyes reminded Ray of far too many psychos he had met during those previous summer months. She had listened to Yarbrough's show like they had. He had found another true believer like Lenny and Billy.

"Yarbrough was insane," he said. "My cousin stopped him when he found out what the Y Signal was really doing. It was messing with people's brains, and Yarbrough was selling them on a false world that didn't exist."

"It was what?" Kristin replied. "What's a Y Signal?"

The lights browned again, this time almost extinguishing entirely. The longer the song went on in some ephemeral crack in reality, the darker it got out, and the harsher the static pitched. He tried to form words to tell them to turn it off, but his tongue refused to work. Instead, he clutched his temples and fell to his knees. Kristin ran over as the cashier stared blankly ahead.

"So it wasn't just a show," she said. A wild grin slid onto her tired face. "This is happening because your cousin stopped the broadcast. This whole time I could have been someplace better."

"Becky, stop talking and help him up. Wait, where is that sound coming from?"

Ray tried to call out, but he could say little as the world drifted away like a specter in the night. He felt a hand clasp around his wrist as he fell backwards into a dark pool of ice water, the cool sensation of death extinguishing the pain in the back of his brain.

Whether this was real or not, it didn't matter anymore. Eternal sleep beckoned him down into the abyss of his consciousness.

And then he wasn't in Burroughsvale anymore.

Part Two
Lost at Home

"We shouldn't be here, Andrew," George said, his voice trembling. The old door slammed shut behind the group, sealing them inside. He swallowed his breath. "This place isn't even supposed to be here. It doesn't exist. It can't."

Weight pressed Andrew's shoulders through his winter coat. An invisible force pushed down on him with the sudden heat and a trickle of blood escaped from his nose. "Why is it so hot in here?"

Danny had already removed his winter wear and was running his fingers along the old cracked wood of the building. He wore his tacky green Christmas sweater and dress pants, the same one he had brought to the sleepover. Andrew joined him in taking off his heavy jacket and snow-pants.

"Are you two crazy?" George asked. "Put that back on and let's get out of here. This is some kind of haunted house."

"Can't," Danny said. He shouldered the door. "Feels like an elephant is on the other side."

Andrew didn't reply. The buzzing in the back of his brain had vanished, as did the sound of the wind cracking against the side of the building. Whatever had led them here, wanted them inside.

The lobby before them was vacant, but dilapidated. The wood paneling looked like it was relatively new, as did the oak desks, and yet all of that was overwhelmed by the green growth hanging off everything, like it had been left abandoned in a jungle for decades. Vines, leaves, and brush, all ran across the walls, desks, floors, and ceilings, in no particular pattern. Andrew couldn't even determine a source for this greenery. It was bizarre enough that it was here in December.

Between this and the heat, he began to think they had somehow stumbled into a jungle. How one could do that in the middle of Christmas vacation was anyone's guess, but yet here they were.

"We're dead!" George whispered under his hard breathing. "This isn't possible. We're actually dead."

Danny quietly stepped beside Andrew and scanned the greenery. "So you two really were telling the truth about that Y Signal thing."

"We were," Andrew said, blandly. "But I don't know what that has to do with it. Yarbrough's definitely dead. Whatever is causing this isn't him."

George threw off his coat and snow-pants, forgetting to even put his boots back on. He ran over to Andrew and shoved him. The taller boy looked down at his frazzled friend in amazement.

"Why did you bring us here?" George asked. "Do you want to die? Whatever happened to *Andrew doesn't go where Andrew isn't wanted*? Remember that dumb motto? You don't mess with nature, stupid. Everyone knows that!"

Danny patted his friend's shoulder. "Easy, George. You're babbling. No point getting mad."

A rush of guilt flooded Andrew's stomach. He had never even been inside the Y Signal, or heard the broadcast. All he did was see Ray return from it. When he slammed that radio over Yarbrough's head, he never expected it to swallow the psychopath whole either. But that was back during the summer, months ago. Why was all this happening now?

And why did he chase Ray away? He would know what to do here. Perhaps Andrew blamed his friend for everything that happened to them that crazy night, even though no one forced Andrew to go: it was all his choice. Though it didn't explain why Ray wasn't brought here, too. Surely, he heard that static. Andrew paced the floor, searching for some kind of explanation.

Then it hit him: something else *was* happening to Ray. Andrew just couldn't help him.

"This is all my stupid fault," Andrew muttered.

George laughed. "Exactly!"

"Stop being a girl, George," Danny said. He turned to Andrew. "What do you mean?"

"At least, we've got the three of us. Ray's on his own; his parents are out of town. He's got no protection right now."

"Then give us the plan, genius." The venom in George's voice only grew stronger with each passing word. "How do we help *him* when we can't help ourselves? What's the way out?"

"Ray told me that he fell from the sky to get out of the Y

Signal the last time. But that's obviously not going to help here. First, we have to figure out just what this place is, and why it's here at the school. If we can get rid of it then, hopefully, things will go back to normal."

"Normal?" George shoved Andrew once more. This time Andrew landed against the wall, dislodging rotted wood. "We were at a sleepover just before Christmas and playing some video games, and you had to drag us to this place. Things finally felt normal for once. Why couldn't you just mind your own damn business?"

"My business?"

"Everything is fine the way it is, so why do you have to change it? Eh? Tell me."

"George!" Danny yelled. He grabbed his friend by the shoulders and whipped him around to face him. "Stop already! What's your problem? This isn't even about him anymore, is it?"

George's face went sheet white, and he clenched his teeth at his friend. "Everything was fine, Danny. Everything was fine! Then your damn hero here got in the way."

"And it will be fine again! Andrew has he never let us down before. We took the hill back during the last war game because of him, didn't we? He helped us with Joey's gang, too. It'll be fine."

George shook his head. "At some point you're going to have to learn that trusting Andrew, no matter how tough and cool you think he might be, is stupid. But fine, I'll quiet down. Not like whining about it is going to do any good."

Andrew stood back up and slowly moved from his two friends towards the branching hallway at the back of the lobby. Each path remained completely dark and hidden by shadows, only a strange sunlight shown in through the boarded up windows. He turned back towards the front door to find that the same light source was now peeking through the cracks. When did that happen?

Both boys followed his stare and jumped when they discovered what he had. They fell into conversation as Andrew cocked his ear. The wild snowstorm no longer blew. They weren't home anymore.

"We're going to have to explore this place, guys. Hurry it up."

George looked ready to disagree when a low growl rushed through the empty building. The rough and gravely voice pitched up into an awkward howl. The closest thing Andrew could compare it to was some kind of ape.

His two friends paled, sweat dripping down their sheet-white faces as they stared at each other. A shaped stirred in the shadows of the left path, flickering like the light of a candle in the moonlight. George and Danny did not appear to see anything, which made Andrew's decision easy.

"We'll go right," he said.

The other two slunk after him as he departed into the abandoned building. Far behind him the sounds of distant crunching and slurping echoed, like a solid object being cracked open and dug into.

"Do you have any idea where you're going?" Danny asked, his voice shaking.

Andrew didn't answer. All he could do was move forward, and hope nothing waited for them in the darkness.

***

The cold shook Ray awake where a blue sky bore down on him. It wasn't any normal blue sky, however, but one the color of the deep ocean. The stars themselves twinkled as if floating in the sea, rocking like the waves. There was a sun, but he could not see it as the sphere appeared to have some sort of eclipse blocking the real light from behind it—a larger dark blue orb. Nonetheless, visibility somehow remained perfectly clear. He sat up and rubbed his sore skull.

That was when he realized someone was holding his left hand, their grip oddly tight. Kristin Oliver sat beside him, also watching this strange new sky staring down through the broken ceiling.

"You alright?" he asked.

She said nothing, continuing to stare at the state of the world around them.

The two of them were sitting in the middle of a crumbling shop that had once been a corner store. Around them were other buildings just as mangled, looking as if they had been through some kind of long forgotten war. Clouds rolled across the impossibly blue sky as Ray surveyed his surroundings. This was some sort of city, but where was it?

"This isn't the Y Signal," he muttered. "I've never seen this before."

Her grip tightened on his hand as she stared forward, trembling slightly. "Where are we? Where is Becky?"

The store was empty aside from the rubble, as if it had been bombed out. No sign could be seen of anyone ever being in this place for ages. They were alone.

"It's just us?" he said. "What happened? And why are you holding my hand?"

"Because when I let go, this happens."

She loosened her grip on Ray, and a wave of pain rolled across his brain. A dark pit emerged before him with static filling his thoughts. Kristin faded out of existence like a bad dream, leaving him alone in a swirling vortex of sound beating at his sore brain. The thoughts of wanton murder and destruction washed through him, causing him to howl out. Darkness encroached on him, hungry for blood and bone.

Suddenly, she grabbed hold of his hand again, and the world steadied. His eyes watering, he looked upon her as the world refocused again. Somehow, their contact was the only thing keeping them weighted to existence in this place—whatever it was.

"Did you see it?" she asked. "I went back to the store, and it was empty—everyone gone, even you. But as soon as I touch your hand, I'm back here. What's happening, Ray?"

He held back a breath before slowly letting it out again. That awkward buzzing in the back of his brain subsided, as did the winter cold. Instead, a sudden warmth ran through him like desert wind. Ray removed his winter clothing as the girl kept talking. There was no snow here.

"I'm not entirely sure," Ray replied.

"I—well," Kristin said. "Ever since we started sixth grade, rumors have been saying the reason you and Andrew were ignoring each other is because you were involved in that radio broadcast last summer. The last time it aired, you two were spotted riding your bikes alone late after midnight, which is weird enough. But two out-of-towners were arrested outside your cousin's apartment after he disappeared, and one said he chased two kids off the balcony. What were you doing out there?"

A cannon blast filled the air. Ray dropped to his knees, his dress pants ruffling in the dirt. The girl landed beside him, covering her head with her spare hand. But the loud bang didn't appear to be close by. In fact, now that he thought about it, it didn't sound like a cannon, but a *gun*. Another shot went off, then another. Someone was firing like a madman out there.

He peered out the cracked window. A flood of people fled down the empty midnight street. They wore rags, leather jackets, and jeans, among other odd, dirty clothing. Were they the ones being shot at? No, the shots went off streets away. Nonetheless, there were other people here. Ray exited the building into the night of this dark city, the girl tagging behind him. They sprinted the city streets.

"Where are you going?" the girl asked.

"If we're in the Y Signal," he said, "then Lenny has to be close by."

The sweltering heat reminded him of the summer, but the empty city was more like the apocalypse. Burned out cars, broken buildings, and that endless crystal blue sky behind the fast rolling clouds, told him that he wasn't in Burroughsvale anymore . . . and probably not even on Earth.

"Ray!" Kristin shouted. "Look!"

Lying in the middle of a sidewalk, a corpse lay on its bleeding stomach, eyes wide and open, blue moonlight reflecting from the unmoving form. Ray's gut lurched in his throat, and Kristin turned away. This guy was definitely not getting up again.

"Is he really dead?" she asked.

A shot went off again. Ray looked to his left to see the very building this poor sap had fallen out of. The second floor window had been broken, clearly where the dead man was thrown from. Inside, more blasts rang out. He needed to shake his fear off and get running.

"I don't think Becky is here," he said. "We should go."

"Now, hold on," someone said. "Don't be in such a rush."

Three men in dirty garb, black clothing and masks over their head, approached from across the street. Ray couldn't make out any expression or difference between their dirty appearance. The trio approached casually, hands in their pockets. He instinctively backed up, the girl behind him.

"Bringing your girlfriend to a neighborhood like this?" the

center man said. "What a cool guy."

"Where are we?" Ray asked. "This isn't Burroughsvale. Are we even on Earth?"

"Earth?" The man on the left elbowed his pal. "Look, bro. Fresh meat. That's rare."

Ray felt the blood drain from him. "What do you mean by *rare*? Are we in the Y Signal?"

"*The Y Signal*? Kid, you've really lost it. This is the city of forgotten souls, lost to the civilized world. A place where the hopeless roam—or whatever it says on that old statue back at the city limits. Who really cares? What we do care about is what we can get for a pair of fresh-faced ankle-biters who stumbled into our playground."

"So you didn't come here from the Y Signal? You weren't brought by the train? You didn't hear the radio broadcast?"

The man on the right couldn't help but laugh. He coughed and spat on the ground. "They always come out scrambled. Good thing the buyers don't care about brains."

The sound of a shotgun pumping caused the hairs on Ray's neck to stand up. A man emerged from the building that the dead man had fallen from. He wore a jean jacket and matching pants, his boots far more season appropriate for whatever this place was than Ray's were. He aimed the shotgun at the three hooligans.

"Slime-balls," the shotgun man said. "Not two seconds after I clear out one rat's nest do I find cockroaches slinking outside it."

"The patrol!" the center man said. "Book it!"

With his words, the trio bolted off the way they came, disappearing into the alley ways. They wasted no time fading from sight. Eventually, it was just the two kids and the stranger left.

Ray faced their savior, feeling Kristin duck further behind him as he did so. That didn't stop her from speaking her mind, however.

"You killed the man over there, didn't you?" she asked.

"I sure did," he said. He kept the shotgun by his side. "Boy, did you say something about a *Y Signal* a few seconds ago? Did you just get here?"

Ray swallowed the fear in his gut. "Yes, we're looking for her sister. She was taken through the Y Signal, just like we were. At least, I *thought* we were."

"These streets aren't safe. I'll take you someplace we're less likely to be easy targets. Don't worry, I'm an officer of the law." He flashed his badge, a cheap looking piece of silver shaped in an oblong star pattern. "I guess this looks different than the ones you're used to."

He gestured for the two to follow him. Ray obliged, Kristin after him, but both were sure to keep their distance. This guy did just kill someone, after all, and he certainly killed other people upstairs. That was when a possibility hit Ray like a lightning bolt.

"Is this Hell?"

"I get how you can think that. But, no. This occult city exists as a space between Here and There. Sort of like your Y Signal was made to access cracks in reality itself, we were brought here by dark forces. The difference is that *we* didn't come here by choice."

"Neither did my sister!" Kristin exclaimed.

"Tell me about what happened, and I'll see just what the problem might be. But I'll say one thing—this *isn't* the Y Signal, and your sister is definitely *not* here. Why *you're* here, I can't be certain."

The three entered an old rust bucket of a car. The gasoline smelled oddly sweet. He didn't question it as they whipped along the barren midnight streets. The stranger hummed an old tune that Ray thought he recognized.

"How do you know what the Y Signal is?" Ray asked.

"I've seen its insides before. We live in quite an odd universe, you know? If you look around enough, you can find anything in the crevices. So tell me. What are you doing in this nightmare?"

Ray found himself talking so much he hardly remembered to keep some details private. Perhaps he had held on to this experience for so long he could hardly hold it in anymore. Nonetheless, he told him everything from the disappearance of Lenny all the way up until the current situation with Becky. He didn't divulge any names or personal information, including his own, but described the Y Signal as thoroughly as he could. By the time he was done, the stranger had fallen speechless himself.

"That's insane," Kristin replied, her mouth agape.

Ray blushed, almost forgetting she hadn't heard most of it. "Yeah, I guess."

"I'm going to take you to see the old seer," the stranger said. "She can sometimes see clearly between spaces into other ones. But I can't say I'm glad to hear from the Y Signal again. I thought that thing was long dead."

"What can you tell me about it, Officer?"

"It's dangerous. That race of things you mentioned—those ape men. They live between the spaces of reality, and they don't like people. To shut it down, you need to stop it at the source."

Ray's stomach flipped as he thought about Yarbrough's certain demise. "But what if the source is already dead, Officer?"

"Then you've got a problem," he said. "But you don't have to worry about that. There's always another answer. You can call me Loren, by the way. Name's not real, but what is, these days?"

The way their rescuer said those last words made Ray's queasiness worse. Where exactly were they, and where was Kristin's sister? As they drove through the dark the questions only beat at his mind more. But there was one unfortunate reality to it all that he had to accept.

The Y Signal wasn't dead.

***

For some crazy reason, the heat only beat into Andrew the deeper he journeyed inside this abandoned radio station. He muttered those prayers Fr. Vic had told him about as he scanned the dark hallway for any signs of life. It was all he had to keep his mind off of this place. The heavy humidity bore down the further he traveled across this old musty carpeting.

He sniffed cooked meat and blood on the air. The more he progressed the more it strengthened, even though he could see nothing. "Hey, guys. Do you smell that?"

No one answered.

"Guys?"

He turned around and, even with his lack of visibility, realized his friends were gone. Fear caught in his throat as he struggled to swallow. A sudden scream in the distance summoned cold sweat on his back. A howl broke the quiet.

Andrew sprinted forward. His quickened pace allowed his pumping legs to take him through the black of the building faster than he'd ever ran before. Ragged breaths didn't stop him his racing mind from thinking of certain death. He needed to forget the smell, the sounds, and the sight of this place. He needed to get out!

And yet, the more he ran, the more his head pounded and the darkness warbled as if a fever held him. A high pitched squeal buzzed in his brain. Andrew rubbed his eyes and found a harsh light suddenly pouring into the boarded windows. Andrew peeked through, his breaths caught in a tangle with his nerves.

The greenish white jungle stared back at the boy. Trees taller than this old radio station towered over rolling brush. Vines strewn across thick branches stuck out everywhere. The humidity punched him even harder through the sealed window. Upturned dirt lay all over the base of each trunk and in nearly invisible trails that spun off into the endless foliage. Chirps cried from close, and even further out roared some large beast. The longer he stared out that broken window the more it hit him that this place was real. It could only be the Y Signal. Ray's dream world did exist.

As he looked out into the white light of day that somehow shone outside the window, a thought bored into his mind. This had to be Yarbrough's revenge. Who else could cause this bizarre place to exist?

The buzzing in his brain hit a fever pitch. He squinted and held his temples as the hum eventually fell away. The growl cried out once more, but this time it wasn't coming from outside.

He turned around and saw it—a seven foot man shaped like an ape, covered in long black fur. There was a face underneath all that hair, but it wasn't that of an animal's. Andrew could barely make it out, but the general shape and the lights of the eyes told him it was a man, or something close to one.

Before the boy could manage to react, the creature slunk towards him, its massive frame loping awkwardly in his direction, no emotion on its obscured face. The ape-man howled a strange whine.

Andrew ran down the hall, as fast as he could manage. The creature screeched as it bolted after. The boy tore forward, his legs struggling to keep the pace he needed, sweat dripping down his neck. He twisted down the hallways like a maze, hoping for a way out.

The hard breaths of the ape creature grew closer and closer, and under the exertion were words. Andrew couldn't make them out, but he knew they weren't gibberish. They made sense to someone other than him. The beast pounded against the floorboards as it it drew closer, even as he turned down the corridors of this abandoned radio station. How many halls did this place have?

As he twisted down one pathway, an arm grabbed him. Andrew found himself dragged into the empty room. The door shut behind him, leaving the small space in darkness.

Outside in the hall, the ape-man continued mindlessly forward, its hard steps crashing against the old floor as it moved onward. A loud bang as if it ran into a wall shook the entire building. Regardless, the ape-man panted hard as it bolted past the room and into the distance. Soon enough, its presence all but disappeared. Andrew was alone with whatever dragged him in this place.

"Andrew!" Danny said. It was so dark that Andrew couldn't even tell where his friend was. "I thought you were in front of us. How did you fall behind?"

Somehow, time and space worked differently here. Perhaps he was affected so deeply because he had been near the Y Signal before. He wiped his sweaty brow. "This is definitely the Y Signal."

A sudden bloodcurdling scream filled the silence of the radio station. It didn't take but a second for both boys to acknowledge who it was.

"They got George," Andrew said.

"Who?"

"*I don't know.*"

The howl of the ape-man overtook George in the distance and a chill caused Andrew to shiver. Now he was definitely of their location.

"This is the Y Signal," he said. "Ray dreamed about this building."

"How do we get out, then?"

Memories of that disgusting force that pulled Yarbrough out of existence while he cried bloody murder returned to Andrew. His teeth chattered, and it wasn't from the cold that should have been here. The winter of Burroughsvale was long gone. Now they were trapped in a nightmare.

"I don't know. Ray just woke up. We don't have that luxury."

The sinking feeling in Andrew's stomach was matched only by his growing regret. If only Ray were here. If only he didn't chased his old friend away. Andrew had no knowledge of this place aside from what his friend had said. Why didn't he take him seriously?

Unlike Danny and George, Ray had actually seen how Yarbrough died, just like Andrew did. The terror on his face as he was dragged out of reality would probably never leave their nightmares for the rest of their lives.

Andrew's legs gave out, and he landed to the floor on both knees. A different sort of cold burrowed into his chest, and an obvious truth dawned on him. There was no way out of a dream if you weren't sleeping in the first place.

The Y Signal would devour them all.

Part Three
Avoiding the Swerve

The officer led the two children into the abandoned tenement that looked like every other hollowed out tenement in this blown out city. They drove here for what felt like hours, but the blocks of buildings went on forever in every direction. The sounds of traffic echoed very far away where the city lights shone far more brightly, but here it was nothing but the silence, and whatever waited in it.

Ray kept his hand securely fastened to Kristin's palm, but she squeezed much harder on him. Trickles of blood seeped out. He decided to keep his uncertainties about their situation to himself.

After the junker of a car pulled over and the three left it towards the crumbling building, the officer named Loren directed them to the front steps. Loren brought out his shotgun, loaded some shells, and grabbed what appeared to be a bag of them at his side. He took the lead, putting the weapon to his chest and walked in front of the group, as if hiding the gun and ammo from their sight.

"How old are you kids?" Loren asked.

Ray decided to go for it. "We're in sixth grade. Last year before we graduate Elementary."

"My condolences." Loren lead them through a barren foyer towards the stairs. The smell of sour milk amidst wet stone assaulted them. "The next few years are going to be terrible for you."

"Really?" Ray asked. "How do you know that?"

"It's always the same at that age. I'm sure you heard a lot of crap about these being the best years of your life. That's more likely to be the opposite, and I'm saying that as someone currently in a place like this. Watch your step, by the way."

The empty building looked like it had seen much better days. Cracks in the brick and plaster ran deep, and the steps of the trio echoed with each push up the metal stairway. The smell of overcooked meat arrived on the wind. He didn't want to imagine its source.

"*Ray,*" Kristin whispered.

Ray leaned in. He let some distance fall between them and Loren. "Yeah?"

"I've been thinking about the Y Signal. Who was the guy that created it?"

"Lenny got in over his head and involved with a man named Yarbrough. He led him in."

She perked up at the name. "Yarbrough! That's the guy from the band my sis loves so much. She's been weird long before all of this, but this summer, she suddenly got very depressed not long after those guys were arrested in your cousin's apartment building. They were really fighting over this Y Signal thing?"

"Yeah, and like all the other out-of-towners hanging around last summer, they disappeared after the Y Signal stopped. Probably because their escape was cut off."

"Escape?"

"The Y Signal was going to bring them all to a new world, or so Yarbrough said. The people that didn't make it are probably really mad about missing the train."

"Why would my sister want to escape?" Kristin asked, no longer whispering. Loren slowed down for them to catch up, and she seemed it used the opportunity to change the subject. "She gets good grades, and she's been talking with Mom and Dad about college. Moving across the country or whatever. That's stupid. College gets you anything, right?"

"You're a bit too young to understand," Loren interrupted. "Sometimes, some people just gotta get away, and they don't care who gets taken with them when they go."

"She always keeps to herself. How were we supposed to know that?"

"If she was anything like I was as a kid, she's probably stupid. We tend to not think about tomorrow and then act surprised when our choices mean tomorrow might not ever come."

There was much that Ray still don't know about the Y Signal, including why so many were tricked into worshiping it, but he did know that they *chose* to get wrapped up in it. Lenny's friend Billy had willingly left to go the Y Signal as well. He chose to leave it all behind. Even without factoring in Yarbrough's nonsense, there was much Ray didn't comprehend about this whole thing.

However, the Y Signal he experienced was also much different than this place. The unseasonable warmth, the dark blue skies, the random whiffs of burnt meat and wet paper caught on the light breeze, all told him he was far from home, but nothing was as off-kilter as that radio station or the train Lenny had boarded during the summer. This place felt *realer*, more tangible, in a way.

So, then, where in the world was he? And how did he get here?

As Ray pondered the questions, Loren led them to the top floor of this blown out apartment complex. There were many squatters along the way. They all kept huddled to the corners, avoiding eye contact with the three of them. The trio eventually ended up before a blown out unit where Loren knocked on the door once. It creaked open.

"*Come in, Officer,*" someone whispered.

Loren leaned back to the two kids. "Give me a second. I have to have a talk with some friends of mine inside. Don't go anywhere, alright?"

The friendly officer disappeared into the apartment and left Ray alone with Kristin and his thoughts. The door slid shut and left them alone on the muggy floor of cracked concrete. At least, there were no squatters in this area. After not even a second after Loren's departure was Kristin was on him again.

"Why did you stop hanging with Andrew?" she asked. "I always thought you were friends."

"We were," he said. "*Are.*"

"You could be more clear, you know?"

"Things have been weird since the summer ended. George invited both Danny and Andrew over for the weekend, for a Christmas party I guess, and I just couldn't go. I keep thinking about the things we saw. Andrew probably does, too. It's hard."

"Sounds dumb," she said. "Friends are friends. Hang out with him. Go play football, or whatever it is guys do. We're graduating soon, remember? We aren't going to be kids forever."

"Thanks for the reminder. Why do you care, anyway? It's not like we've ever talked before."

"Well, you know." She paused, glanced at their clasped hands and then the musty carpet. "You guys aren't the most approachable. The rumors don't help."

"I thought it was because of your friend Bridget. She's always calling Andrew a dumb ape and the rest of us his chimps. Always thought that was because he beat up her boyfriend that one time."

"Marco wasn't her boyfriend, though she probably wishes he was. They both have big fat mouths that never stop talking. Anyway, my point is that this isn't the time to beat around the bush. We should act before we lose the chance, right?"

They were in sixth grade, that much was true. But the passage of time wasn't that concerning to him. He kept thinking of darker things, things that had haunted him since the summer. It was what lay just out of sight that kept him up at night.

"Do you ever get the feeling that things aren't quite right?" Ray asked. "That when you go to bed that there's a globe out there still spinning, and things are happening in the dark where no one can see them? It's like the world is changing on its own, and we just go along for the ride hoping we don't fall off. We can't steer the ship or even jump to a new one. You know what I mean?"

She raised a brow at him. "You read too many *Goosebumps* books, Ray. Things aren't that complicated. Work hard, go to school, get a job, and raise a family. Life is not tough."

"And you read too many *Babysitter's Club* books." Visions of Lenny in that restaurant returned to him. He knew he would never forget that disheveled sight. "If there's one thing life isn't, it's simple."

"And you'd know? We're the same age!"

The thought of Yarbrough waiting in the dark to pull the boy down into that dark hell he was cast into flashed as a possibility in Ray's mind. The last words of Lenny came back to him, as did the look Andrew gave him when Andrew then said he didn't want to hang out anymore. All of that happened in less than a week, and it changed everything. He made the wrong choice somewhere along the line, and it was too late to fix it.

"Sometimes, I wonder," Ray said.

The apartment door swung open. Loren gestured at the two kids to follow him in. "You two are going to need to keep calm when you see this. No overreacting, okay?"

Ray closed the door behind them. "How bad could it be?"

"You're about to talk to someone who is almost dead, but not quite alive. She's going to say some strange things, and she isn't going to look right, so be prepared."

Loren left down the hallway, his shotgun still at his side. Kristin looked after him before glancing at Ray, a question forming on her open mouth and curved brow.

All Ray could do was shrug. "Guess we're about to see how simple life really is, eh?"

***

Andrew hugged the wall. His breaths fell hard as the sweat dripped from his neck. Danny stared blandly at the closed door of the empty room as Andrew managed to finally get himself off the floor. The stench of blood was ever-present.

Thoughts of that thing that pulled Yarbrough through the apartment floor last summer filled Andrew's every thought. It had returned to take him, he just knew it.

But George had nothing to do with this, neither did Danny. Andrew had brought them both to this place, against their wills. He swallowed hard as he tried to think of how to get them out.

Danny hissed between his teeth. "Tell me what is going on here. What is the thing in the hall?"

A jolt of energy fueled by indignation gave Andrew the will he needed to speak again. "I'll get him back."

"Did you see that thing out there? It's huge, easily over six feet, and I don't even just mean its height! Nothing should be that wide. We're just kids. We can't do this!"

"Shut up, and stop whining. I'll do it."

Danny jumped forward and shoved his taller friend. Andrew hardly expected it and lost his balance, landing against the wall once more.

"No, you won't," Danny replied. "George was right about you. This was our last chance, and you screwed it all up. Why couldn't you leave things alone?"

"You're so stupid, Danny." Andrew stood over his shorter friend. "All you ever do is fight to solve all your problems. Do you really think picking one with me is going to solve anything now?"

"How else are you ever going to pay attention, idiot?"

"Pay attention to *what*?"

"You need it spelled out for you? George is moving."

The fire suddenly left Andrew and a harsh cold gripped his insides. "Moving?"

"One of the reasons his parents allowed us over was because

this was going to be one of the last times we were going to hang out. He's leaving after New Years. He just told me the other day. We couldn't even get Ray to come because the two of you are such complete idiots."

"He could have said something about it. Ray and I would have listened."

Danny rolled his eyes. "George isn't like that, and you know it. He wanted it to be normal, and you two, in case you haven't noticed, have gotten really bad at being that. No one knows how to talk to either of you anymore."

Andrew's legs had almost failed him again, but he managed to retain the adrenaline he needed to force himself up. He shouldered past Danny towards the door.

As much as he might have messed up, he still couldn't let it mask what he had to do here. In fact, now he had to act more than ever before. If they were going to die anyway, at the very least, Andrew wouldn't do it cowering from that freak of a monster. George needed him. He had a life to get back to.

Andrew put his fingers on the doorknob when Danny seized his arm. The shorter boy's fingers trembled as he held tight.

"Where do you think you're going?" Danny asked. "Want to offer yourself as food?"

"Something like that."

"Everyone at school is right. You really are a complete moron."

"What else am I supposed to do, Danny? Wait here until I die of old age? Escape outside into that jungle and hope whatever is out there doesn't kill me instead? I don't even know if I can get us back home, but I can at least find George. If this is the Y Signal, then we are in serious trouble no matter what I do."

"If it wasn't for you and Ray . . ." Danny bit his lip. "Things were going so good, you know? First he started going on about things not feeling right—"

"Was he wrong?"

"I don't care if he was right! Things were fine. They were always fine. Don't you get that?"

Andrew jerked his arm free from Danny. He turned the doorknob and charged out into the hallway. "Maybe they never were."

This winter hadn't been the greatest. Andrew's parents had been arguing again and were headed back for counseling. It didn't look like they would walk out of this one intact. He didn't want to think about it. At the same time, the guys at school were walking on eggshells around him. On top of it all was the fact that he would be graduating sooner than later, and then he had those creepy dreams all the time. Perhaps a part of him blamed Ray for all of this, but Andrew did know better about this than Danny or George did. There was more to this than any of them really understood, and this was his chance to find some answers.

He slunk down the hall with careful steps, Danny nipping at his heels and whispering harshly under his breath. A howl slipped down the hallway from the north. He made his way towards it, dodging the broken glass and busted drywall carpeting the dirty, cluttered floors.

"Are you crazy, Andrew? What do you think you can do against monsters?"

He didn't have an answer, but whatever he tried would be better than dying alone and huddling in the dark. He still had friends to find.

***

The torn-up apartment unit didn't have any intact walls, and Ray couldn't help but stare out into the unending sprawl outside the window of this hovel. The night sky prevented much in the way of visibility, especially without street lights, but this city appeared to go on forever into the deep blue horizon. Kristin appeared to agree, as she mumbled under her breath while she also overlooked the endless view. This place was far from Burroughsvale.

Loren waved a hand in front of their faces, then pointed to the floor. "She's here, kids."

Sitting in the middle of this old building, on an old carpet was a white-haired woman with a blindfold wrapped around her eyes. Her scarred legs were folded over as she leaned against one of the larger chunks of the rubble. Despite the color of her hair, she didn't look any older than Ray's mom or any of her friends. The blind woman looked up at them, and Kristin gasped.

"Is this who you were talking about, Officer?" the woman

asked.

Loren nodded. "Yeah, they just showed up in the middle of town during a siege. They say the Y Signal sent them. Can you tell why they're here, Kelly?"

Blood streaked like tears from under the blindfold across Kelly's pale cheeks. "I already saw them arrive, officer. Arrivals are hard to miss when you get so few. Why are they holding hands?"

"How would I know? Kids are kids."

"We can't let go," Kristin said. "When we do, we disappear. We can't leave until we find my sister."

Kelly turned from Loren to the two kids as if she saw them all clearly. The old woman paused in thought. She licked her lips as if allowing what to say form in her mind.

"I'll be frank," she said. "The girl you're looking for isn't here. She's being guided by the Y Signal you know so well. You can't reach her from here."

"That's ridiculous!" Kristin shouted. "Of course, she's here. We went through the same thing she did. Where *else* would she be?"

Kelly stretched her arms, allowing them to crack. "That's simple. She is where that boy would be right now if you let go of his hand. The two of you are keeping each other anchored to this place. I can't know all the details, but it seems like the Y Signal is calling out to those who heard it one last time. Since you've never heard it, Missy, it has no power over you. And yet, at the same time, it is pulling at whatever it can as if desperate. To balance the two of you out, it looks to have sent you both here as a compromise. These are higher workings I can only guess at."

"Some compromise," Loren said. "So all they have to do to go home is to let go of each other?"

Kristin looked from Loren to Kelly, confusion dawning. "But if I let him go, he'll end up in that dark place. I can't do that. He might be able to find my sister, but what if he can't get out?"

The decision Ray would have to make was becoming all too obvious. He had few options between staying in this limbo world glued to Kristin forever, thereby keeping her in constant danger, or letting go and risking another plunge into the Y Signal. This thing would never let him go until it was destroyed. He couldn't avoid the obvious decision forever.

"That's where your sister is," Ray said. "I can get her."

"That's crazy! You don't even know if she's there. We don't even know if this old lady's telling the truth. How do we even know this isn't some kind of hallucination?"

"We would be so fortunate." Kelly cleared her throat and wiped some of the blood dripping onto her lips. "Here is the best I can figure, children. I do not consider myself an expert, by any means, but I can share what I believe. Between the tangles and strands of life, exist other fabrics inside. There are spaces you can't normally touch, taste, hear, smell, or see. That is, unless the boundaries are bent. If there is one trait that human beings are known for—it's bending rules as far as we can before snapping them in twain. The Y Signal is such a thing. If you wish to stop it, then you will have to stop it at the source. Unless the boy goes, you will never see your sister again. Believe me or not, it's up to you."

A loud bang erupted downstairs. The building shook, and Loren tripped against the wall. Gunfire went off, and a cavalcade of steps poured in down on the lower floors.

"Another raid party," Loren said. He pumped his shotgun and headed towards the door, his bag of shells rattling beside him. "You kids better go quick. It's going to get messy very soon."

Kristin looked Ray over, her brow furrowed. She clearly didn't want to ask him to do what she secretly wished he could, but how could she could approach the subject? He couldn't blame her for fretting about her sister, when he still worried over Lenny. Nonetheless, keeping his classmate here was endangering her life for no reason. He would be in danger no matter what his decision was.

"Thanks for your help," Ray said to Loren and Kelly. "I just want to know one thing. Do you know what the Y Signal actually is? How do I stop it for good?"

"Wake the source up," she said. "It can only operate as long as one can power it."

"I thought I already did that?"

"The Y Signal will eventually die on its own, as all signals eventually do, especially those thriving on unnatural sources. Dive into the darkness, and make certain the one behind it is thrown from the seat of power. From what you say of your situation, it's time is already running low. But you will have to hurry. If it dies with you inside, you will be trapped there until the end of time."

"Hurry it up, kids," Loren said. He leaned on the hallway

door frame as steps rapidly beat up the flights. His shotgun steadied, he watched his corners. "Make up your minds already."

"Already did," Ray said. "I'm going."

Kristin went wide-eyed. "How will you even find her in that dark?"

"If it's too tough, I'll call out, and you can grab my hand and pull me back. How's that?"

The last thing Ray wanted to do was go back in there, but he had little choice. This whole Y Signal business was his responsibility, and it had wrecked his relationship with his friends and taken his favorite cousin from him. Now it was threatening both Kristin and her sister, and probably others. For all he knew, Andrew was under assault, too. After everything he had gone through with this thing, he couldn't just walk away.

Kristin must have agreed because she slowly nodded at his statement.

"I'll make it fast," Ray said. "You'll see."

The boy let go of the girl's hand and stepped away from her. The world swirled as if a spin-cycle had gone off around his head. Gunshots fired somewhere nearby, death screams rattled, but he could see nothing aside from the warped figure of Loren shooting out into the rapidly vanishing hallway.

Eventually, the voices disappeared as if they were flushed down a drain, and the sight of physical existence faded away from him. All that remained was a black universe. The cold enveloped him, but it was not that of the winter weather.

He tried to reach for his arms to huddle closer, but he could not seem to touch them—in fact, he could not feel his arms move at all. His chest had also disappeared. He neither saw nor felt his own body. Ray's panic grew as he struggled against nothing while he drifted alone in the void. The boy was not a physical being anymore, all his senses dead and gone aside from the cold that held him tight. He might not even have been alive, for all he knew.

Loud buzzing split into his stray thoughts, and he winced, or *tried* to wince. Whether he even had eyes or a brain to feel or see any of this was unclear. It creaked and whirred about the abyss as static in a radio tuner, searching for a sound. Eventually, a loud discordant guitar chord cut into his very soul, splitting it open.

"*Welcome home,*" a static-filled voice said. "*We've been*

waiting for your return."

The squeal of the feedback pitched higher and sent shockwaves of agony into his being. He tried to call out, but there was no voice to yell.

And then existence itself simply turned off.

Part Four
End of the Line

Ray should have died. Maybe, he did. It wasn't so much his eyes that opened, but that Ray's perception of space became tangible to his being. Suddenly, he was aware of his surroundings in a panoramic sense where he could take everything in. What he was aware of, however, was not much he could have described even if he wanted to.

The boy found himself in a dark tunnel that rolled on to infinity before and behind him, with no clear exit in sight. A floating patchwork of what he thought were windows strewn about the open space took his attention. They all hung askew as if part of invisible houses that had been tossed about in a raging tornado. No walls existed for them to be attached to, and they were in fact not connected to anything, despite the fact they floated like hummingbirds deciding where to take in their next meal. These window-like squares of light also hummed, though it was closer to a dying radio tuner than any sort of animal. Only the sight of faded white snow—or was it television static?—appeared in those floating spaces.

Ray tried to step forward, but he felt no legs moving underneath him. Nonetheless, he found his perspective shifting as if he was walking under his own power. Each window appeared to bend to face him as his body-less form moved past them. They were like stars dotting the eternity of outer space.

"Andrew! I hear breathing in here!" someone said.

One of the windows let another voice respond to the first. *"George is still alive then?"*

"Yeah, but we won't be if we go in there. What are we supposed to do?"

The voices whirled around Ray's thoughts as he appeared to be involuntarily pushing forward. Were those his friends? He attempted to gaze around the tunnel but found only more endless dark.

The more he scanned this place, the more he became convinced that the tunnel was not actually a tunnel at all, but far closer to a kind of tube.

What he thought a ceiling was instead a sea of black with stars dabbing the eternity surrounding this existence. They faded in and out of view like lamp lights whipping by on a late night car ride.

Blurs of various colors passed by, almost like taillights rushing through the black of night. A low chorus of voices sang somewhere just under the static burst filling Ray's being. The more he tried to focus, the more he was certain one of them was a girl he had met before. Kristin's sister? They were all drifting along this narrow road to whatever lay ahead.

"*Danny!*" Andrew said. "*Help me out!*"

A part of Ray felt a pull towards these voices. He let it stretch, and his corporeal form grew as if water spilling across an old kitchen table and seeping into the cracks. A portion of him moved towards the static fissures while the rest mindlessly flew onward. He couldn't stop either part from doing what it wanted, mostly because he didn't know what *he* even was anymore. It was like losing one's bladder control as an infant or not knowing how to crawl. Whatever he was supposed to do was beyond his comprehension.

Instead, Ray let himself split apart. Wherever he went, that would be where he would end up. Existence fractured as he thought of his friends waiting just out of reach.

He was a part of the Y Signal now, fading into the ether.

***

"What is that thing?" Danny whispered. "It has George."

Andrew shushed his friend. They had finally found that oblong ape carrying George under one of its massive arms. The monster took a hard left turn—and walked right *through* a door as if it were a ghost of some kind.

The two boys stared for a moment at what had just occurred. Andrew placed a hand over the very door the monster had passed through. For a moment, he thought the ape-man had melted the very material around the old wood, since it was discolored—only a vague black imprint of the ape remained on the slab as if cut out. However, the stain suddenly formed itself whole again, the old cracks even returning to where they once were moments earlier. It was like the monster had never walked right through the physical object to begin with.

Andrew went for the doorknob. It was cool to the touch, but he could still turn it.

"Andrew!" Danny said. "I hear breathing in there."

"George is still alive, then."

"Yeah, but we won't be if we go in there. What are we supposed to do?"

But what choice did they have? George was dead otherwise. Andrew steadied his breathing and wiped his brow before he opened the door.

The barren room hadn't been used in many a day. Aside from the light slipping through the boarded-up windows, only the dust and cobwebs among all the rotting desks and bent chairs showed him that this room was once in use. Nonetheless, it remained empty aside from the ape man carrying their friend across the abandoned office.

"Danny!" Andrew said. He found some hunks of stone amidst the rubble and scooped bits of it up. "Help me out!"

Danny flashed a glare like he was about to argue, but a roar cut from the monster him short. The ape man gripped its forehead, and a burst of static echoed throughout the room. The unexpected explosion of warm wind nearly knocked Andrew back and actually did push Danny down. Andrew could swear he recognized the voice screaming on the air but wasted no time, using this opportunity to sprint forward. The ape-man stumbled as it clutched its skull.

Andrew caught George by the elbow and dragged his friend free of the ape-man's loosened grip. The beast spun around and struck the tall boy with its palm. Andrew and George both rolled backwards against the dusty floor, knocking through the rubble littering this place. The ape roared after them.

The queasiness stirred Andrew's brains like stew, and warm blood flowed from his nose. As he scrambled to stand up, his legs bending in every odd direction, stones flew over his head and bounced uselessly off of the ape-man's hairy chest. It gazed up at Danny and his futile attempts to distract it.

"Get away!" Danny said, his voice shaking. "Go back where you came from!"

The beast leaped over the junk pile, passing over George and Andrew. It tromped towards Danny, beating its fists against the floor. Its jaws clenched as it moved, saliva spilling out. Andrew shouted for his friend to run, but Danny froze in place doing little but staring at the approaching ape-man with his mouth agape. He clearly knew he was dead.

Heavy air suddenly punched the atmosphere like a sonic boom, knocking everyone in the room over. A figure glided through the shadows, and the space rippled around it. This walking shadow, highlighted by a white outline, as if snipped out of another time and place, approached the weird ape. No concern or care dawned on his face, and neither did any acknowledgment that he was approaching another being that shouldn't exist before him. The barely visible boy sunk into the monster's body as if he were a ghost possessing a hapless soul, and disappeared from sight.

The ape man howled as its flesh and skin crackled and popped. Steam burst from its insides, and black blood leaked from sudden holes opening across its reddening skin. Bangs erupted from inside. It was as if it were being shot apart from its interior.

Regardless, the boy walked entirely through it and passed the three stunned boys. The barely visible child crossed the room towards the door before he disappeared through that, too. Something about his stride looked familiar.

Andrew blandly stared after him. "Ray?"

"Look out!" George shouted.

The ape man screamed and danced about as if it were set aflame. Steam and blood continued to gush out of the monster's boiling body. It fell over itself as if not knowing what to do. Danny dodged a wild swing of one of its massive arms before turning towards one of the boarded windows. The thing didn't even seem to know he was there as it approached him.

An idea popped into Andrew's head. "Guys, the window! Push him!"

The monster screeched, though it did not appear to see them as it frantically rubbed at its open wounds. The three boys ran from behind and shoved the monster towards the window. It pinwheeled its arms in its lost balance, tripping into the solid wood of the boards before it.

The ape man slipped through the boarded window, just as it did the door earlier, passing through the very material itself. The foreign sun shone in the room as the boards burned away with the monster's touch.

For a moment, it seemed as if it would just phase through, unmolested. However, it instead solidified and cried out. The wood, and shards of glass on the other side, became caught in its shifting form. It screamed not unlike a train whistle breaking through the deep silence of night. An explosion of wood and glass caused the ape man to screech, piercing Andrew's brain as black blood splashed out of the thing's broiling wounds.

The three boys dropped to the floor, avoiding the shattered window shards and sprayed splinters of wood and life force. The ape man's voice faded away as the bloody mess fell from the window.

The ape man hit the dirt, shaking the ground. The corpse bled out into strange earth before it began to melt, seeping into the dirt like a shallow puddle. It soon disappeared from sight as if the jungle itself had claimed the beast. Only the stench of sulfur filled the air.

"Its gone." Andrew left the window for the door. "I'm sure that kid was Ray."

"That wasn't him," Danny said, his voice trembling. "Couldn't be."

George swallowed hard before speaking, his face caked with sweat. "Let's just leave."

The three boys exited the room in silence. That ape man never returned, allowing Andrew to breathe easy for at least a few seconds. That is, until he saw what was in the next room.

In the center of the small space was what looked to be an old recording booth for some sort of radio show. Andrew didn't know anything at all about broadcasting or whatever it was those DJ guys worked from, but he assumed it must be close to this. Greenery and plants overran the broken glass of the booth, and the consoles and equipment were rusted beyond recognition, made it appear that this area hadn't been used in a long time.

And yet, in the center of this abandoned place, sat a lanky man in a busted desk chair, clutching a microphone in both hands. Jeans shorts, a ratty band shirt, and dreadlocks made him look very familiar. He appeared to be sleeping, aside from the fact he was muttering into the mic. That was the moment Andrew recognized this guy from Lenny's place back during the summer. He was the one the cops arrested outside Lenny's apartment, the guy who chased them from the building. This tired punk didn't flinch at the three normal kids, but he did look up at the specter of the young boy.

"Don't I know you?" the punk asked. "You should be entering the Y Signal right now."

"No, Brad," the specter said, his voice filled with the pops and crackle of static. "The signal is fading. Unless you turn it off now, a lot of people will be trapped in the void, stranded and alone."

"What do you know about the signal, boy?"

"More than you. You are living off the last sparks of the Y Signal. Yarbrough is gone, and without him, you can't do anything."

"You!" the punk exclaimed. "You're that kid—you were at Lenny's! Where is he? I can't wait to see the look in his face when I come strolling in to the signal. I'm finally gonna get away."

Ray's ghost shook his head. "You might have taken over Yarbrough's game, but you're not him. You're just screaming into the microphone, hoping for it to work. Unless you turn it off now, we will all die, Brad."

"Ray!" George shouted. "What is going on with you?"

The ghost didn't look away from Brad. "I'm between spaces. It's not going to last forever. Once Brad turns the signal off, it'll all be over."

"No!" Brad shouted. Spittle escaped his flapping maw. "I'm not going back! I'm going to where Lenny, Billy, Andrea, and everyone else is. You can't take that from me."

"Yes, I can," Ray said.

"Stay back! This is my signal now. No one has the right to be turned away."

Ray's ghost reached out and gripped Brad's forehead with both hands. The stunned man's eyes widened as Ray's fingers sunk into his brain. "Sorry, Brad. It's done."

A hard burst of static cracked the air like lightning with drums of thunder rolling around underneath the rising whistle slipping into the atmosphere. Andrew covered his ears and flinched back, as did his two friends.

The static field sent cold chill through Andrew's bones, covering basic visibility with winter mist. It took a moment for him to realize that it was the snow itself. Both Brad and Ray were consumed in a bright white light consumed by the intruding weather. Within a moment they were both gone.

That light spread like a bomb going off, swallowing all else in the room. The last thing Andrew heard were the screams of both George and Danny at his sides before the world went white.

Then the cold returned.

Frost bit at Andrew's cheek and rose him from his slumber. The falling snow of the blizzard chilled his skin and caused him to jump back up. He was alive?

The night blizzard whistled loudly through the empty snow field. The radio station had vanished, leaving him alone in the night with the distant Christmas lights shining. He was home again?

A coat landed on him. It took a moment to realize it was the exact winter jacket he had taken off earlier. Danny crouched next to Andrew before handing him his gloves.

"I found them getting buried by the snow," Danny said. He gestured to George, who was sliding on his own coat. "We all need to get out of this place. Hurry up."

"Wait," Andrew said. He couldn't help but notice that they were the only three in the field behind the school. "Where's Ray and that Brad guy?"

Danny put his gloves on. "Not here. They were probably just some kind of hallucination."

"You don't know that." Andrew forced himself back up. "We should look for them."

"Look *where*, Andrew? There's no one here! It's just snow everywhere. Let's just go back to George's before we freeze to death. We'll call Ray in the morning. You'll see, he'll be just fine."

Andrew couldn't puzzle out what Danny was doing. Had he lost his mind? Ray had just saved them all. They needed to find him. What if the Y Signal got him? Aside from the three of them, there was nothing but the squall to be seen. All traces of the radio station was completely gone.

"Where are you going, Danny?"

"I already told you. It's late, and you dragged us out here to the middle of nowhere. I'm not going to die in the snow in the middle of the night for this nonsense."

Danny didn't waste any time as he rushed towards the gate by the school and disappeared into the storm. His speed was impressive considering how deep the snow was in the field.

"Forget it, Andrew, there's nothing to discuss." George stepped beside Andrew and offered him his hand. "It's over now.

Let's be thankful for that."

Andrew stood up with his friend's help. "You alright, George? Did that monster hurt you?"

George's lip trembled. He pulled his hood down further over his head and masked his eyes. "I don't want to think about it. We've got to go back home before my 'rents notice we were out."

Perhaps it really was all some kind of dream. Either way, it was over, the jungle was gone, and now they were in the Burroughsvale winter again. There was nothing left to do here.

The pair left the barren field behind. As they walked through the tall banks with the wind fighting them, Andrew asked the one question still on his mind. Perhaps it would also take George's thoughts off of what had just happened to them.

"Danny told me that you're moving."

"Yeah."

"Why didn't you tell me?"

George looked at Andrew then back to the road ahead, pausing for a long time. "I wanted to keep the good times as long as I could." His tone hardened. "That's over, now. Once we move, I am never coming back here again."

The icy words struck Andrew deep in his chest. He didn't know how to respond to that assertion when he felt much the same. He'd seen things no one should ever see, nor should anyone have ever dabbled in this insanity. It wouldn't be the same again, and he knew that deep down.

Andrew tried to change the subject. "You think Ray is okay?"

"Assuming he was even there? Yes."

"Really?"

"The four of us are roaches. You're going to need a lot more than a nuke to wipe us out."

"That's an intense way of looking at it."

"Well, who knows what's out there, right?" George cleared his throat. "I figure being able to survive is the same as winning, isn't it? I know that's what I'll be telling myself the next time I go to sleep. If I ever do. That's what we get for getting involved in this sort of thing. Some things are meant to be left alone."

Ahead of them, Danny waited on the sidewalk as the blizzard wind blew against his smaller frame. Andrew waved to him, but his friend did not wave back.

"Are you going to be okay, George?" Andrew asked.

George didn't look at him. "I don't know."

The three friends walked through the streets of Burroughsvale, silence surrounding them just as the unending snowfall did. It would be days before they would speak to each other again. Andrew became so focused on their troubles that he didn't realize the headaches had vanished, never returning.

And yet, Andrew couldn't help but wonder, deep in the recesses of his mind, if this was all worth it. Had they really won anything here? Even if the Y Signal was gone, and Ray was safe, what else was waiting out there in the dark?

Ahead of them, Danny mumbled to himself as they crossed the barren streets. "*Turtles in Time* or *Contra 3*? Which one should we play first? We've got plenty of time before sunrise, I figure."

They did not know at that time that it would be the last game they would ever play together. With that frosted winter night, so ended the world they once knew so well.

***

"You look like you've fallen down the stairs," Granny said.

Ray had walked back into the apartment, fatigue weighing him down like an anchor. Ever since he stepped through those cracks in existence, he felt the energy sapped from him. It took all he had to walk back here. He waved to his grandmother as he locked the apartment door behind him.

"Feeling any better, Granny?" he asked.

"Yes. I don't know why, but I feel refreshed." She stretched from her position on the couch. "You go to bed. It's not good for you to be up all night. Your parents would kill me if they saw this."

He smiled at her. "Sure thing. Good night, Granny."

"Before that, lovey. Don't take your parents going on this trip with your brother to heart. They mean well and want to do best by him. We do get to spend Christmas vacation together. They'll be back soon, and things will be normal again. You'll see."

"I know."

"Have you been practicing your painting?"

"Yes, Granny."

"Good," she said, snuggling back into her blankets. "We'll paint tomorrow, okay? Get some rest and feel better. It will all be better in the morning."

He could only smile back at her. For a reason he couldn't understand, tears welled up when he tried to form a sentence. Ray wiped at his watering eyes.

"Are you sure you're well, Ray? You sound like you're coming down with a cold."

Ray cleared his throat and wiped his brow. "I'm fine."

The boy left her there, at least a bit happy in the knowledge that the Y Signal appeared to finally be gone. He put away his winter clothes before stumbling down the hallway to bed.

The blizzard rattled the windows. He rubbed his sore head, massaging the bridge of his nose.

"Why couldn't you leave it alone?" Kristin's sister had said. *"We were finally going home."*

Ray had just finished calling the police, directing them to the convenience store. The sirens could be faintly heard through the howling snowstorm streets away. Kristin had watched her sister sitting on the floor beside the unconscious form of Brad. She did little except smile at Ray's arrival when they all landed in the empty shop beside her. Her older sibling would not stop crying.

"Thanks," Kristin said to Ray. She embraced her sobbing sister. *"Becky is stupid, but she'll get over it."*

Her sister sneered at them. *"Get over what? You took us from paradise!"*

"That was no paradise," Ray replied.

"And this is?"

"It's the best we got. At least, you have people who care about you." He glanced at the slumbering form of Brad, and then thought of Billy. *"We aren't all that lucky."*

The boy had seen through the cracks, whole places and people and things most others would never come across in this lifetime. The Y Signal, or what remained of it, no longer led anywhere at all, if it ever had in the first place. It was broken, dead like Yarbrough was. Brad had been left blindly leading them to annihilation, or worse. They wouldn't go wherever it was Lenny ended up, and it didn't look like Lenny was ever coming back. They would all live on here, like the rest of them.

Ray tried telling Becky that much, but she wasn't having it. The girl just ranted and raved like a loon over things he didn't understand. It was yet more madness and whining. Ray used the excuse to leave. He had reached the limit of dealing with these teenagers, and he doubted he would ever get them. Kristin bid him goodbye as she consoled her sister, leaving Ray to push through the blizzard back to Lenny's old apartment where his grandmother slept. It was a long trek with his sore bones.

Now all he could think about was that pure anger on the older girl's face. Brad's insanity, the desperation Billy had displayed months ago, and Lenny's disappearance, all would continue to stick with him. What was it about them that irritated him so much? Why couldn't they accept the way things were? Was it an adult thing? Was he too young to get it? But then, his parents were not like this at all. In fact, they were overjoyed in the possibilities his younger brother had for the future. Things were always getting better, and they always would.

Wouldn't they?

Ray slunk into bed in the same room Lenny once used before he vanished into the long-gone Y Signal. He pulled the blankets over his sore skull, attempting to ignore the cold winter knocking on the window. Nothing had changed; everything was normal again.

As he slowly slid into slumber, he thought of his friends. They were there in that building with Brad, weren't they? It was difficult to remember everything. He had barely seen anyone other than Brad through the haze of static, though he remembered moving as if he were part of it. But that sensation had already become a forgotten memory. It was as dead as the Y Signal now was.

If Andrew, Danny, and George, actually were there with him then they were surely as free as the others. Unless he imagined their presence to begin with, that is. Either way, he would call them in the morning; when the night was over, and he could put this storm behind him forever.

The last thing Ray saw before he slipped into sleep were Christmas lights still shining outside in the blizzard of the night, somewhere far away from here. They were always there, reminding him of better times and better days in another world, another time separate from this moment. Electricity or not, Christmas was coming.

Time still rolled on.

He might never see Lenny again, but at least he still had the days and years ahead of him—however many that might be. Tomorrow was always another chance, especially now that the static in his head had cleared.

The lights twinkled in the vanishing haze inside his tired mind. Christmas was almost here, and he was home again. Things were as they should be. He would remember that single moment of warmth and comfort under the covers for the rest of his life.

1995 was over, and he wouldn't have it any other way.

YOUTH'S LAST SPRING

You remember the last thaw of the last winter before graduation, even if your memory doesn't. You wake as you always do, carry the same backpack you always carried, and feel the same breakfast in your stomach you always ate, but you knew something was different. It stuck in the back of your thoughts—you knew this would be the last stretch before you left it all behind.

The cold gave way to a warmth, but not the one you knew so well since those days you played in the rain puddles with your best friends. You are much too old for all that now.

But you weren't too old to forget the way things were, the uncertainty ahead hanging over you like the clouds gathering before a storm. Little did you know how much this would stay with you long after these days would be forgotten by the rest of the world. It wasn't the same for them as it was for you—for them, it was just another day.

And yet when you stepped into the school on that brisk spring morning, the chill no longer stung as hard it did in the winter months. You could tell that it was almost over.

You smiled to your friends, hung out as you always did, sat awake in class and waited for the bell—and you knew that it would stay this way forever. At least, this feeling will stick with you over the years. It is a part of you, this joy that comes and goes like the very seasons passing you by.

But it's all over now, and you know it. Everyone knows it, but they will never say it—not when you need those last precious moments to keep you warm before the end.

You remember the last thaw before graduation, and it sticks with you every time the winter gives way to spring. This only occurs once, but it happens all the time.

This is your life now. From now on, the spring will be different. Deep down you will always know that, even as these years behind remain little more than memories. Raise your head high and look ahead. What awaits when the chill finally breaks and the sun's warmth swallows you whole? What does winter lead to?

One day, the cold will never return, but you'll still have the memories. And eventually, they will be enough.

Endless Summer

Part One
Going Underground

"Pizza has all four food groups, Ray. That's how you know it's good for you."

Ray's father kept his hands on the wheel as he pulled into the *Rustik* parking lot. He did not pick a spot, instead idling in front of the front door to the restaurant, though it wasn't like the boy expected his old man to stay. It was only his oldest son's graduation party, after all. Graduating sixth grade was not that big a deal.

"Did you hear me, Ray?"

"I heard, Dad."

"You did good today, so have fun in there. We'll come get you at closing time. Are you going to be okay on your own?"

The graduation ceremony had gone about as well as expected. Each kid had their name called and walked across the narrow stage, some gathering more applause than others, wearing their dumb formal clothes they wore under their gowns. Their parents probably bought them just for this occasion, though Ray's parents were no different in that aspect. And now, here they all were, the after-party at the fanciest restaurant in town. Though considering that town was Burroughsvale, it wasn't saying much. His folks, however, would not be joining them. They had other appointments.

His parents sat in the front seat of the black Volkswagen, with his young brother at his side in the rear seats. The little runt kept busy playing on Ray's old Game Boy and didn't seem very engaged in the situation. He kept sighing and looking out the window in his usual fits of boredom. Ray's urge to smack the idiot grew with every passing moment. But today was supposed to be a good day. Why ruin it over dumb stuff? "Can you really not stay?" Ray asked.

"We've got to get to the Ferguson party," his mom said. "They do work for the bank, after all, and they know certain people. Your brother is going to get quite the boost when he finally starts at Loyola Elementary in a few months. He's going to have all the advantages we wanted to give you. You can always get some pictures for us. Besides, like your father was just saying: we'll have a small party of our own next weekend. It's a win/win."

"Yeah, sure, Mom."

Ray exited the car, and his parents quickly turned around in the lot. They waved as they disappeared back onto the main street of Burroughsvale. Ray felt an odd bit of anxiety as he watched them go, almost as if he would never see them again.

The boy quickly put it out of his mind and ascended the steps to the *Rustik* restaurant. Those nerves twisting in his stomach made him grimace. No matter what he did these days, a chill would slide down his spine at a moment's notice. It had been half a year since he dealt with the Y Signal at Christmas, and a year since he had last seen his cousin Lenny last summer. New dreams had taken the place of those memories as the days had gone on, showing him visions of a paradise that didn't—*couldn't*—exist. Every time he woke up, a part of him seemed to be missing. At least today, he could get some respite from his own uncontrollable imagination.

The *Rustik* was the only fancy place in town for adults with too much money and spare time. There weren't many other spots like them. It was mostly for the richer families, but Ray had heard about it from Ant and Frankie before. He recognized the drink fountain (today with soda, of course) and the carefully decorated round tables littered about with white lace over the top. The sound system played rather low, choosing a Smashing Pumpkins song he had heard too many times. All the other kids from sixth grade were there, wearing their best suits and dresses as if they were going to a wedding. Even though he wasn't any different, he couldn't help but think it odd. Was today really that big of a deal? The teachers and many of the parents were also in attendance and chatting amongst themselves by the bar. They floated over the plain grey carpets to fetch kids to drag into their dumb adult conversations. They looked like they were more excited than the graduates who, like him, appeared to think it just like another day in class, as they goofed and chatted about the TGIF block. No one really acted like it was the last time many of them would ever see each other again. There would always be tomorrow.

Ray sat at a table in the far corner, near one of the six foot tall windows. No one appeared to notice his arrival, and that was just fine. He didn't even know why he was there. School was over. What was to celebrate? They had passed other grades before. How was this one any different? Was it because they randomly decided kids should move to a new building? Adults could be dumb.

"Hey, Ray," Kristin said. She approached from a nearby table and stood beside him. The girl wore a white dress that definitely matched her braided blonde hair well. Not that he knew much about fashion—his own navy blue suit looked dopey. "I didn't think you'd show up."

He gestured for her to sit beside him. She obliged. "I am wondering why I did."

"What do you mean? Aren't you glad to graduate?"

"I guess. Not like I wanted to fail. No one does."

"Then what's the prob?"

"I don't know. I guess it just doesn't feel real. I keep thinking that it was just yesterday that I last saw Lenny. He's just gonna come waltzing out of that bathroom over there and make a dumb joke before he orders his meal. But that's not going to happen, because Lenny is probably dead."

Kristin bit her lip and glanced over her shoulder as if making sure they weren't being watched before she leaned in closer. "You probably heard rumors about my sister, right? She ran away last week. Never even left us a note."

"Do you think—"

"The Y Signal? No. She got into a fight with my folks, then took off. It's weirder that Andrew came up to me yesterday to ask about her. He wanted to know if she'd had any dreams before she disappeared. I told him that I don't know, but she usually talked about that sort of thing. She kept a dream journal, as lame as that is. Andrew's your best bud, Ray. Why was he asking about my sister?"

Ray forced a smile and shrugged. There wasn't much to say about Andrew. Ever since what happened at Christmas, they had started talking more and more, but it wasn't the same. Looking each other in the eye became difficult, like they didn't want to acknowledge an uncomfortable truth they both knew. Ray understood his friend's issues—he had heard from George what they had seen that night before Christmas—but he didn't know why he couldn't speak to anyone about it. Andrew had started dating one of the girls in class, and Ray had been hanging around Kristin more and more, but none of the guys could really keep it together anymore, especially after George moved.

"I have been having weird dreams recently," Ray said. "Not like the old ones: I've been seeing a place. It looks like *here*,

Burroughsvale, but it's not. I don't know how else to say it. Feels like the way things used to be. Where are Andrew and Danny? They keep dodging me about this stuff."

"Danny and Andrew are talking in the hall by the bathrooms. Better go quick before one of them hits the other, like when they came back from March break."

Ray sighed and rubbed his forehead. "Those two . . ."

"Always fighting these days. Good luck, Ray. You're going to need it."

"Are you alright, though? I know your sister meant a lot to you. Maybe she's just goofing off because it's summer. Don't teenagers do this a lot?"

A faint smile appeared on her lips before fading away. "Maybe in the movies. I'm fine, though. Go talk with your friends. You're not going to have much time left to do that, just like me with mine."

"You sound like an adult."

She laughed, waving him off. "I'll take that as a compliment."

The rest of the party appeared rather oblivious to him as they did each other, but that is how it had been since the school year started. Rumors had a way of replacing truth for some. He left them to their devices as he sought out his friends.

Before graduation, there were announcements over the PA system warning about dating and holding hands at recess, and some of the other kids were causing trouble with the seventh graders at the school down the hill. It was as if they were already primed and ready to leave this world all behind already. The teachers giving serious talks to the other sixth graders was more and more common.

Oddly enough, he couldn't quite buy it. Nothing had changed.

Ray had caught many of the other kids wistfully embracing nostalgia for the good old days, whether it be remembering ascending the north stairway to visit the library for the first time, or waiting in the gym in first grade to get your class and teacher assigned to you, or the first recess they experienced. Weren't those memories just a few years old? Ray's first grade teacher had already forgotten his name, so perhaps those days would be lost sooner than he thought. Either way, there was an unspoken sadness among the rest of the kids no one really wanted to express with each other.

Maybe he had just imagined it, just like those dreams.

While the chatter of adults and his peers went on in the party room, Ray found his way through the wide halls of the *Rustik*. In front of the bathrooms, he found his old friend Danny sitting on the floor, gazing at his dress shoes. The grey suit made him look much older than a sixth grader, but it was the look on his dull face that showed he was just another a kid at a party. He pouted at Ray's approach.

"You," Danny said. He ran his fingers through his slicked back hair. "You've done enough."

"Enough of your stupidity, Danny. Where's Andrew?"

"The basement. Says he's been having dreams. I told him to let that garbage go. George is gone, and we're never going to see him again—he told us so himself. Now we're graduating, and all of this is going away. It's over. We're going to be the same boring teenagers as those stupid seventh graders always causing trouble. Studying, girls, part-time jobs, and then we graduate and become our parents. What a waste."

"You've been thinking about this a lot." Ray had been, too, though when he woke up randomly at four in the morning for the first time ever, a fear of the unknown kicking at his gut and an inner voice told him that everything would change forever, he didn't believe it. He couldn't. But everyone sensed it, even if they didn't want to admit the truth. These days were ending, and what was coming did not have much in the way of promise, just like Lenny had told him. Was the Y Signal right? "I've been thinking, too. But at least, we can have some fun until then, right? I'll get Andrew, and it'll be just like old times."

"Without George, why bother?" Danny stood up and brushed at his pants. He passed Ray down the hall back towards the party. "I hope you're proud of yourself."

Of all Ray's friends, it was Danny who reacted the worst to the whole Y Signal business, creating a rift between them all that had only grown wider with every day. He kept to himself these days. Ray didn't expect that would change in their new school, especially considering Danny's growing anger and violent tendencies. He never used to be a constant in detention. Things had changed.

The basement door Andrew had apparently entered was

still unlocked. Ray made certain no one was watching and entered. He found it particularly odd that there wasn't much staff around today, though perhaps it had something to do with the fact that a group of graduating sixth graders were simply not that much to handle. Compared to the new arrival of first grade kids causing problems this past year, Ray's class were angels. At least, that's what the Principal said at the school assembly about the growing bullying issue. Regardless, those kids were the future of the school—Ray and his peers were destined to be forgotten just like the previous set of sixth graders were at the end of last year.

At the bottom of the stairs, he found a veritable cavern with tables and plastic and wooden chairs stacked up to the unnaturally high ceiling. It was like a maze down here—he couldn't even see the edges of the room. Cold sweat ran down his back. What was Andrew doing in here?

"Andrew?" he asked.

Ray called out to his friend, but the echo was carried away into the dark. His own voice reflected back at him, someone harsher and gruffer as if it had aged forty years in a split second. This place was beginning to make Ray's nerves twitch. He bit his lip and pushed his way through the tables and chairs, tension in his muscles harder with every passing moment.

"*Andrew?*" his voice echoed.

Ray's call reflected back at him again and again with increasing frequency and power the more he forced his way through the dark, as if he were answering the questioning phrase himself. Ray body checked some chairs and nearly fell over as he tripped over them. They rattled against the voice.

"*Andrew?*"

The sound of water lapping up on the shore poured into his brain with every second he spent down in the basement. Ray squinted his eyes and smacked his cheeks. He walked in a circle to find he had no idea where he was in this sea of old furniture. No walls existed here. His exit had vanished.

"*Andrew?*"

He ran forward, crashing through anything he could, hoping for anything to remind him of reality once again. The waves rushing in his mind continued in frequency and volume to where he could no longer hear anything else. Ray ducked his head and barreled onward, desperation causing his breaths to fall harder and the sweat on his brow to nearly blind him. He wiped at it as he attempted to ignore the insanity around him. Where was he?

"*Andrew?*"

"*Andrew?*"

"*Andrew?*"

"*Andrew?*"

A burst of static in his soul swallowed the world. The basement disappeared, and so did his consciousness.

When Ray opened his eyes, he found himself landing onto his face. Red jabs of agony prickled at him. He slowly rose back up, brushing himself of the dirt and dust from his precious suit. His parents would certainly have yelled at him for this one.

But when he looked up, he found no familiarity with his surroundings.

Ray awoke in a dirt tunnel that had clearly been dug by hand, or possibly primitive tools, which winded onward and backwards into the dark. The only reason he could see was the torchlight beside him which carried up stone steps into what looked like an unfinished basement. Ray came out into exposed pipes and insulation with some vents in the ceiling for good measure. The long basement led him to a set of small, unfinished, and empty rooms, all coated with cheap wood paneling.

He would have thought it a normal house if not for housing an actual jail cell at the rear. This small space had actual steel bars, even on the slit of a window that allowed sunlight in.

The lone prisoner sat in a pile of rubble that filled the cell, leaving him leaning against the wall with only his scarred chest and upper body showing through his crumbling clothes and out of place stone chunks. The half-dead man laughed when he saw Ray approach.

"The other one now," Yarbrough said. "Just in time."

It took a moment for Ray to recognize his old enemy fully. The dirt and crust and the creases on his face along with scuffed up hair made Yarbrough look like those homeless people that New York was filled with before the news said it was cleaned up. But those were different times. The world was moving past that sort of thing. His parents always told him they were moving to better days ahead.

Yarbrough coughed from his position on the cluttered

floor. "You thought I was dead, right? So did the people here. When I showed up, they freaked out and threw me in here. Thought I was going to take their dream away. Well, they're half-right."

"Did you bring me to this place?" Ray asked.

"Thought you might have been at least a little older. We've been here for so long that time doesn't really have any meaning anymore, though it still does. You'll see."

Ray cocked his head in an attempt to understand this. The last time he saw Yarbrough, the former member of the Paranoia Agents had been dragged through the floor itself by whatever was in that radio Andrew broke over his head. That was a year ago, but Yarbrough looked much older somehow.

"Where is my friend?" Ray asked.

"Upstairs. I suggest retrieving him quickly. If not, you might never find your way out again."

"What do you mean?"

Yarbrough shrugged. "You wouldn't understand. You're the only one left who can stop this now. Think of it as a dream that will turn into a nightmare if you don't wake up. Get that?"

A growl filled the air, and a shadow moved out of the corner of Ray's periphery. He turned towards it but found nothing else in the basement. Silence returned.

"What was that?" he asked.

When Ray faced Yarbrough again, his old enemy had completely disappeared. The cell vanished as well, leaving only the empty basement. No trace of Yarbrough remained. It was as if he had never been there to begin with.

Ray found the stairs up out of the basement. He wasted no time ascending them to the next floor and putting Yarbrough out of his head. Andrew couldn't have gotten that far ahead of him, not when Danny had just been speaking to the boy mere moments earlier. They needed to get out of here fast. The sunshine soon met Ray at the top of the stairs.

This house had floral wallpaper, shag carpeting, and popcorn ceilings, not unlike the ones many of his friends' had in their homes. He couldn't quite understand why this place looked so familiar yet so alien. Had he been here before?

The boy stepped outside into the sunlight and found a park across the road. It was full of kids his age and younger playing around on swings and jungle gyms that looked as if they had been recently built. The grass, too, was bright green and short as if it were also being properly taken care of. On the park benches and tables sat the older teenager boys and girls making out with each other, and further than that, adults gathered around in a circle like it was some kind of big party. Despite them, there was a plentiful amount of old cars like station-wagons and Oldsmobiles running down these familiar suburban streets.

These strangers all wore old clothes—striped shirts, plain jeans and skirts, and even some had their hair piled high or sprayed in place. They looked like kids from the 1980s, of all things. It was like one of those teen gang and romance movies he used to rent on Lenny's recommendation.

Warmth permeated his thoughts, allowing a sense of serenity and long-missed certainty inside. All his anxiety faded as he walked the streets of this town that loved him.

Ray reached the road where the sunshine baked him alive in the summer heat, and the distant car rumbles from the streets reminded him of summer vacation. The street names were foreign, as were the faces he spied around this unfamiliar town. The lack of shadows along the grass solidified that uneasy feeling he had since coming here.

He wasn't in Burroughsvale anymore.

He was home.

Part Two
Forever Summer

Ray woke up smiling. Summer was always the best time of the year, and this summer was no different. Warm weather, endless freedom, no school, friends and family at your fingertips, and a new adventure every day. This was the way it was supposed to be.

The boy could only feel gratitude for his town. The streets were full of kids, those he knew, and those he had never met but someday would. His cousins, aunts, and uncles, family he thought had died—all turned out to be alive! Everyone he could think of was here and living their lives. The summer sun beamed down eternally, letting no shadows spoil the mood or the perfect warmth. He spent so much time outdoors that he hardly noticed when the red sunset made itself known to tell him it was time to go home. But he didn't need to return back to his house in this place! The night came and went in a blink, and the days continued onward forever. It was endless summer here.

Ronnie and Johnny brought him to the creek where they caught frogs for hours before Ray's brother found them. The shrimp told him his grandmother wanted to see him. Normally, Ray might be annoyed, but there was always a tomorrow here, not to mention he had never known his very young brother to be so talkative. It was almost as if they were the same age. On the way to the farmhouse, they chatted about everything from their upcoming trip to where Ray would be going to school next. For the first time, it felt like they were on the same page.

For the first time since his grandmother died, Ray painted again. It was good that she was here. The colors swirled in pastels, leaping from his mind to the canvas. She chuckled, praising his determination to trace out an endless summer. He had almost forgotten the joy she exuded when painting, inspiring him even further to get it right. Every day was like this—something he loved, something exciting. This was summer as he always knew it.

Sometimes, he thought he saw a shadow ripple a bit, on the rare occasion he spied one, and the night spoke whispers of things he couldn't perceive, but they always faded away. The dark had no control here, try as it might. This was how it should be.

During one of the few times Ray ended up at dinner, his parents had flat out asked him the choice he never thought he would get. Should they use his father's week off spending time with their grandmother in the country or their uncle's place in the city? It was a wide open decision, and Ray didn't want to pick. Instead. he flipped a coin. They could always visit the other one next year. There would always be time.

At the arcade, he rubbed his eyes on his striped t-shirt. Was that Shawn over by the *Sunset Riders 2* machine? Ray's old friend leaned over it playing with Chris and Andrew. Ray approached, and the group gave each other high-fives. It felt like ages since they had last seen each other. Didn't Shawn just come back from visiting family overseas? He couldn't remember. It didn't matter.

"TGIF is back on tomorrow," Shawn said. "My uncle is a producer on the new show *One of the Family* and got me as one of the extras for the classroom. You guys gonna come over and watch?"

Chris laughed loudly. "Of course, man. Too bad Jay's out of town! I bet he'd love it."

"I didn't know they made a sequel to *The Simpsons* arcade game," Ray said. "I thought they would never make one." He ran his fingers along the freshly scrubbed cabinet. A bunch of teenagers were already at the Camp Krusty boss and shouting at each other for help. Mr. Black looked really tough fighting from his hydrofoil. "Wasn't the last Simpsons game that really bad SNES one?"

"Don't know what you're talking about," Shawn said. He slipped his red cap onto his towheaded mushroom cut. "I gotta go see my granddad now. You guys keep it up. Remember TGIF!"

Shawn exited the arcade, and Chris wandered away to the *Mortal Kombat 4* machine (the one with backgrounds like an old Shaw Bros movie!) to play as Smoke again. Thankfully, he was human once more and not a dumb cyborg anymore like in 3. Midway fixed that stupid mistake. Things should always improve, after all.

Ray turned his attention to Andrew. His taller friend was busy trying to beat the first boss on a biplane. *Sunset Riders 2* sure looked crazy. "Andrew, how are your folks doing?"

"Fine."

"They get through counseling alright?"

"What counseling?" Andrew nearly missed his jump and swore. "They're fine like always."

"Really?"

"Yeah. Something wrong, Ray? You're sweating a lot."

A thought bit at the back of Ray's mind, like he was forgetting something. A familiar guitar riff played over and over, echoing like a train whistle deep in the distance. He scratched at his neck when a familiar name suddenly popped up as if springing out of the ether. When was the last time he saw his cousin?

"Where is Lenny?" he asked.

"Uh, I think he's at our school. He hangs out there during the summer for some reason."

Ray thought about school, the time he and Andrew used to climb the fences—the one time they threw a rotten banana peel they found onto the road, and a speeding car that wasn't there seconds earlier somehow got hit by it. Thankfully, the driver was going so fast she didn't even realize it smacked against the roof until much later. The announcement on the speakers warning kids to be more vigilant was funny, but there were more kids than just Ray and Andrew there. Was it Chris and Shawn? Ronnie? Corey? Steve? Emmett? Johnny? The faces of his friends were right there in the fog of his mind, but the names were just out of reach. Why weren't they here now?

"Are your 'rents still thinking of moving?" Ray asked.

"Are you kidding?" Andrew smiled as he watched the defeated boss fall from his biplane. "Summersvale forever, baby. We got everything we need here. Jobs, schools, neighborhoods, and some cool stuff like these games coming in all the time. Why go anywhere else? Anyway, where are Danny and George? They're missing this."

Ray blinked. Those were the names he couldn't remember! "Right, where are they?"

"Who?"

"Danny and George. You just said their names."

"No, I didn't."

Ray stared after Andrew for a moment. His old friend paused for a second and ended up getting his character Bob killed in level 2 and losing his last life. Andrew turned around and barreled towards the arcade's exit as Ray stared flabbergasted after him.

Too many bodies crowded around the entrance for the new machines coming in, blocking Andrew inside the arcade. Instead, he rushed out the side fire exit. Ray trailed after him, slipping through the packed crowds of kids and teenagers. The two of them spilled out the rear of the arcade into the alley, Andrew ignoring him as he made his way towards the street.

"What's going on, Andrew? What's wrong with asking about Danny and George to join us? Aren't they our friends, too?"

Andrew stopped in the center of the alley. The old musty brick was cool in the shade between the buildings, the summer sun arching overhead. This felt like the only place in town where shadow existed. No one would be coming here except to pick up the trash—and today wasn't garbage day. Crowds of youths flooded by the alley exit where the street lay, but none looked into the dark. Why would they? There was nothing to see here on summer vacation. Even Ray questioned why he was there. That didn't stop him from going in on his friend.

"Why aren't they here?" Ray asked. "Why doesn't anyone seem to know them?"

"Because they ignored the call, Ray. They can't come here, unless you want to go out there and bring them here yourself. You wanna do that? You wanna leave? I don't think so."

Ice suddenly frosted inside Ray's veins, and he shuddered involuntarily at the notion. Andrew was correct. Leave this place? Why would he leave when he had everything here? No one sane would ever do that.

"But it doesn't make sense, right?" Ray asked. "Everyone else is here, even our parents. They didn't seen any of this before, did they?"

"Don't question it."

"You aren't acting like yourself Andrew. This isn't you."

Andrew spun around and punched Ray in the face so fast the shorter boy didn't have a moment to react. He landed against the side of the dumpster, the resulting ring reverberating through the alley. Ray's eyes rolled a bit in his head. He wiped the blood from his stinging nose.

"It doesn't matter, Ray! *That* place—whatever it was—is gone now. No more insanity, no more endless fighting, no more stupid adults screwing everything up, and no more leaving. It's exactly what it's supposed to be. Summer is right again. This is how it was always meant to be. You know it even more than I do. Why would anyone ever choose to leave this behind for a sad imitation of the real thing? Don't start with your questions when we already have all the answers. This is home!"

That was when it hit Ray so hard that he thought he'd been punched twice. "Yarbrough was right. I didn't imagine meeting him. This is wrong. It has something to do with the Y Signal."

"Shut up, Ray! The Y Signal is gone. It died last winter."

"No, that's not what I mean. This is the place the Y Signal was leading everyone to. This is where Yarbrough was taking all those people who couldn't go back home. People like Lenny and Billy. Yarbrough did lead them to that Promised Land. It's here."

Andrew shrugged. "He might have been crazy, but he was right. So what, Ray? What do you plan to do about it? Do you even know how long you've been here? How many days? Do you even remember the nights? I don't. They blur so fast it's just like when I was a kid again."

"You still are a kid, Andrew. You should enjoy what time you have left."

"Shut up! Don't give me that adult garbage. If I have to hear that one more time . . ." Andrew balled his fists up again, shaking quite a bit more than he was earlier. "This is a miracle, as far as I'm concerned. Everyone here is safe, healthy, and happy. That's all that matters."

"Yarbrough is dying," Ray found himself saying. He didn't even know why he said it or how he knew it. That song playing in the back of his head reminded him once more of his old enemy in that cell. "He warned us about staying here. Something is wrong. I believe him. We have to find Lenny and get everyone out of here."

"Then go find him yourself. I haven't seen him once since I came here, and I don't care if I ever do. Now leave me alone, Ray. I've got a date with a seventh grade babe for the second *Judge Dredd* movie. I heard they got it right this time. They always get it right here."

"Andrew."

"Drop it, Ray. For your own good."

Ray called after him, but Andrew didn't listen to his friend. Instead, the taller boy ran back out of the shade and into the sunny streets. He merged into the crowd, disappearing from sight. Ray had never seen him run that fast before.

The cool brick soothed the boy's head as he rested against it. The pain of the bruise subsided for a moment and allowed him to focus. What could he possibly do now? He did not know where he was or how long he'd been there. Was any of this even real to begin with? There were only two people with answers, and one of them Ray couldn't trust—not when he caused all this to begin with. Only Lenny could help him now.

Ray turned towards the road, and dizziness overtook him. He tripped and shouldered the alley wall. A hard spike of pain bore into his right eye like a drill. A headache? Ray squinted, clutching his socket.

When he opened his eyes again, a world of endless night appeared but for a second. The black sun tilted slightly off-kilter like a shadow of the real thing, and the rest of the town became off balance as if melted in a microwave. There were no details to any of it—the town was constructed of nothing but black ash, instead of the brick and wood buildings he knew so well. In the corners, slunk misshapen shadows which ran and hide that looked like . . . apes?

Then he blinked again, and it was all gone. That off-beat existence vanished with the pain he felt in his forehead. The endless summer returned, undaunted.

Sweat poured down his trembling arms and legs through his shirt and shorts down to his sneakers. Ray remembered Andrew's earlier words: Lenny was at the school. He didn't know how much time he had left, or how time even worked here, but he knew that he couldn't wait anymore. That world of dead ash was nearby. It would soon be reality.

The sounds of summer on the streets crashed into his soul like waves on the beach. Children played, car engines roared, and teenagers laughed among their peers. Ray sprinted down the road towards his home, hoping against hope that all of his fears were wrong. Most people loved to be proven right, sometimes even he did, but nothing would have made him happier to be a complete idiot and his fears misguided. This was his real hometown; it was Burroughsvale that was false. Every part of him knew it to be true. He needed it to be true.

And yet as he twisted down the roads, his mind frazzled at the sights. Wasn't the Swidzinski Bakery on the other end of town? Was there really a hill here with a pawn shop beside a tiny grove of trees? Were there always three malls along this highway? Was there ever a highway here to begin with? He didn't remember seeing a clock-tower before . . .

Everything was wrong. But was it ever right to begin with? How would he know?

That familiar guitar riff screeched in his soul again. A sharp pain slashed at his insides. He screamed out and fell to the pavement. Sirens screeched in the distance.

When he looked up again, the sun was setting, and the children flooded from the streets. Out of the corner of his mind, he thought he saw a porch, and with it, a familiar old woman sitting on it as she always did. She called out to Ray, telling him it was time to go home. The sky darkened much too quickly for him to see just who it was in the shadows, but the voice was unmistakable. His grandmother let our her familiar laugh.

"Had enough fun yet, Ray?"

"Granny?" But of course she was here! That was definitely her. Everyone was here, right? "Is that really you?"

The sun vanished from the sky, and for a single moment, just as it always did in the summer, darkness reign supreme. The day was over! Tomorrow would be a new day of discovery, comfort, and camaraderie. For now, it was time to rest.

Never mind the waves of light rippling overhead in the sky like a stone in a pond, tearing into reality itself—that was all normal. For only a second, he thought he saw children, teenagers, and adults, tripping into the dark as if struck by bullets on the front-lines of some faraway military skirmish. Dozens fell. They all dropped, unmoving, into the waves of dark, slurped up into the oncoming night.

Before he knew it, they were all gone.

And so was he.

Part Three
Heart of Flesh

"He's not coming back, Ray," she said from the hospital bed.

Ray ceased playing *Kirby's Dream Land* and put away his Game Boy. Much as he liked the game, it was difficult to concentrate after all that had happened. He looked up from his chair towards his grandmother lying in the hospital bed. The sunset hung in the late afternoon air as everyone else in the family had gone out for dinner. Ray decided to stay here alone with her.

"Granny," Ray said. "Lenny will be back one day. He just has his problems to work through."

She shook her head. "This last week has left me to think quite a lot. I've been having dreams. I see him there."

Ray sat forward. "You did? Where is he?"

"I knew you would believe me." She smiled weakly from underneath her covers. "No one ever believes anything unless they see it themselves these days. But not you. You've changed a lot since last summer. I saw him living somewhere that was just like Burroughsvale, but wasn't."

"I don't get it, but that doesn't matter. How do we get him back?"

"You should be more concerned with yourself, Ray. You know better; you've seen enough. How long will you stay in a world that will never be?"

That familiar guitar riff echoed around the room and slashed his insides. Ray clutched his heart, allowing the pain to ripple by. His grandmother didn't budge at the sound. Did she not hear it? Why did it follow him here? He stood up and found the hospital room was gone.

The boy awoke in the picnic grounds, the very ones he would visit with his family when he was younger. Humidity bore down on him, and he wiped the sweat from his eyes. The barren grove littered with old picnic tables, a vacant fire pit, and the forest surrounding them, reminded him of days he had long since forgotten. Back then, they sang songs, played games, and the town itself could hardly be seen outside during the summer. It was a different time.

As he stood there, the air flickered in waves of shadow, showing him crumbled ash and burned forest in between the familiar sights he knew so well. It was a look into the spaces between reality itself.

"You okay, Ray?"

The voice quickly faded into the silence of the spinning world around him. Did he even know who that was? Were they even a real person? Was anything here real at all? What was reality anymore?

In the waves breaking through reality, vague forms slipped through the ruins of the old world of Burroughsvale into the new world here. These shadows dipped into the corners, hiding behind everything from picnic tables to tree stumps—anything to avoid being seen. And yet, he still couldn't see them, at least, not fully. Nonetheless, they followed him from a distance.

"*You're running out of time,*" Yarbrough said. The musician's whisper echoed across the silence as if added in the post-production of one of his songs. "*He isn't going to last forever. What's taking you? I thought you were serious about this?*"

"It isn't easy," Ray said. He couldn't discern what was real anymore. How did he even get here to begin with? Which was the dream world and what was reality? The past and the future no longer appeared distant, but neighbors to each other in this one moment. How old was he? Where did he come from and where was he going? He shook his head. "Why did you bring me here?"

As soon as he asked the question, Yarbrough's voice disappeared.

What was it Andrew mentioned? The school! Lenny had to be there.

As he walked forward through the spinning world, the sight ahead became clearer—that is where he found that familiar building he more or less lived in for the last seven years of his life. How could he ever forget that place? It was as if St. Willibrord Elementary wanted him to find it.

The same two story rectangular building and open playground he had known for nearly a decade at this point was nearly unchanged, nearly being the key word. The fence that surrounded the yard looked somewhat taller now, especially in that it was covered in barbwire like some government facility out of those old movies. This whole sight was out of place here. Was it the more pronounced cracks on the walls and windows? Maybe it was just that he knew he didn't belong there anymore. Ray approached it with a growing trepidation in his heart, one he had come to know so well.

He pushed through the back entrance of the school. The door whistled a high pitch squeal as if it hadn't been oiled in some time. Humidity rushed out of the school as he forced his way in.

Across the hall from him were the same heavy swinging doors he knew so well, leading to that familiar gymnasium. Memories mixed with comfort flowed through him as he reminisced about those times he passed through here, how it always seemed a bit smaller each time. St. Willibrord was always a relatively tinier school than most, which led to the gym also having a stage for the school plays at the opposite end, but it felt more cramped than what he remembered. Was Lenny really hiding here?

Black patches of dirt and cracks were strewn about randomly in the gymnasium. Wind whistled like an invisible tornado outside, even though there was no storm in this place. Of course he couldn't help but notice the lack of anything else inside these familiar halls. There was no one here on summer vacation, apparently, not even the teachers.

"Lenny!" Ray shouted. "I'm here."

The wind cracked harder against the walls, rattling the windows. For a moment, he thought the building had been blown over. Fog filled the gym as if a steam pipe had suddenly exploded. Ray looked towards the stage where most of it appeared to gather.

The shape of a man appeared in the haze like he were covered in a thin mist blanket, barely masking him from reality. He stood tall at the edge of the small stage, then sat down as if on a throne in some ancient castle. Only shadows allowed themselves to be seen though the fog. The boy faintly recognized this outline of a person.

"Ray," Lenny said. "I didn't think I'd ever seen you again."

"You didn't come back. You lied to me."

"I had no choice. Those people would have been stranded. I couldn't leave them there alone."

"They all look like they're doing fine, Lenny. Granny was asking for you right up until the end. You never came back. She never got to say goodbye to you."

"I'm sorry for that," Lenny said. He paused and sat back in his chair. "It's been a while. I thought you'd all be gone by now. We've been here for ages, you know. Even if everyone looks the same as the day they arrived, much time has passed. You must have met Shawn? He was my first son. I can't leave here and see him anymore, though. If I leave, *they* will break through. They've made enough cracks to this place."

Ray sneered. "Those shadow monsters. I knew there was something up with them."

"Not that it matters what they are. This place constantly gnaws on me, wearing me down. I'm tired all the time now. Eventually, it will win."

Ray froze as he tried to understand the insanity Lenny had just spouted. He couldn't quite get a hold of it, so he chose to approach the only aspect of this situation that he could even slightly comprehend. "Is this town real? Is it the Y Signal?"

"The Y Signal died; this is another space, between the sheets of reality. The signal led us to another world—this place, our new home."

"*Between the sheets*? Is it like an alternate dimension?"

"There is one reality. Long ago, something like lightning fell, and cracked creation itself, sending us slightly askew. Look at the Earth's rotation, and you can get that much. The world you live in is the only purely physical one that man walks in, neighboring the sheets on top and underneath like on a bed. We are not there right now—we are in a place *between*, where man forms the physical *himself*."

Ray shook his head. "Why do you keep saying *sheets*? What does that mean?"

"I mentioned beds. Think of it that way. Earth itself is like a sheet. Physical, understandable, basic. Where we are is a place man was never meant to roam: this is a place our minds cannot quite comprehend. Between the sheets. The Y Signal opened the path, and we took it before it died."

"But it's gone now, Lenny. It's been a year since you left. I'm graduating; the guys are all over the place, and my little bro is starting school soon. Everything has changed. You can come back."

"It might have been a year for you, but time isn't the same here. You might have noticed we don't really have nights—no reason to sleep. There's no telling how long we've been in this place, living free. I have kids now, but I don't really know how old they are. Despite how long I have striven to keep the walls up, and keep them all safe, it's all starting to crumble. You've seen the cracks, right?"

The school certainly did look battered and out of sorts, but it was hard to tell if that was a feature of whatever this space was. That might explain why Yarbrough had sought someone out for help. "I thought this was your Paradise, Lenny? Why are there cracks?"

"I made due with what we had and upheld it as long as I could. There are beings hidden and watching, trying to break through. I can only keep them at bay for so long before my tired bones give out. I'm not immortal; I don't have abilities or powers. My control over this space only exists because I was the first to find it. But that fades as I do."

"You're not really here before me, are you?" Ray couldn't see beyond Lenny's vague shadow, but he could tell that his cousin was a lot more frazzled than he let on. "We'll figure this out together."

"This has little to do with you, Ray. It's my problem. You should go back to your home."

"That's not how it works, and you know that! I was brought here. We're family, Lenny. You know how that's supposed to work."

"But it doesn't."

Ray shook his head. "I'll make it work. Let me in. We'll talk, like we always used to."

A slight pause followed Ray's words. The humidity suddenly spiked, causing the boy to cough uncontrollably. Why was the temperature changing? Was it based on Lenny's mood?

Lenny's shadowed form waved an arm towards his younger cousin. "We'll talk."

Ray slipped into the spreading fog towards Lenny. He leaped onto the stage and stood before his ephemeral cousin. The boy reached out a hand, and his thoughts and vision rippled like a rock skimming pool water. That familiar feedback slipped into his soul like a bad amp in an alternative rock song, ricocheting against his insides.

The world spun, and he fell from it, much like the first time it happened a year ago. He remembered that feeling of helplessness, causing his breath to short as he clawed at the nothingness forming around him. And yet, inside his mind a tiny voice spoke.

"*Open your eyes, Ray.*"

He quickly obeyed, finding himself standing on an endless unmoving ocean with a clear blue sky traveling forever onward in every direction. A familiar town awaited deep below the waves, surrounded by a thin black film. It reminded him of some kind of dark bubble. Was that Lenny's Paradise? He stared at it mouth agape, before finally noticing a familiar young man across from him.

"Lenny?"

Ray's favorite cousin looked up from the water at the boy. He was just as he remembered him, his clothes cleaner and hair kept and cut, but otherwise the same uncertain smile upon his lips. He waved at Ray, a glint of a grin in his familiar tired eyes.

"I've lost perspective, Ray." His voice slurred as if he had either just woken up or got the stuffing beat out of him. It was hard to tell. "Too many people depend on me keeping them safe in Paradise. My sense of reality is bent, and I need you to be straight with me before I lose it entirely."

The underwater city reminded Ray of home, but none of the surrounding ocean appeared to touch it, as if avoiding contact with the forged reality Lenny cut out of this space. Nonetheless, it was then that Ray noticed the water directly surrounding the town wasn't blue, but dark shadow drifting like a fog that beat against the black film of its protective bubble. Slowly, incrementally, it looked like it was seeping into the edges of the city like a leaky dam.

"You really trust me to help you here?" Ray asked. "This is your Paradise."

"You're the only one that's left with a clear head." Lenny winced, rubbing at his eyes. "It's taking all I have even to speak with you right now."

Down beneath the waves, hundreds of children played unaware in the park, teenagers held hands and argued with each other in the mall, and adults sat on their backyard porches by their pools and grills. Not one of them noticed the blackened ocean slipping into their blissful space. Did they even know the water surrounded them to begin with? Those shadows poured in faster with every passing second, causing fissures to the outside dome.

Soon enough, it would break the barrier.

In the mass of bodies of familiar faces, even Ray had a friend. Andrew sat in the movie theater among the crowd, throwing popcorn at the screen and laughing at whatever he was watching. He didn't even seen to remember this wasn't his real hometown. Maybe he no longer cared. Then again, Ray had been there himself.

"Wake up, kid," Yarbrough said. "It's do or die."

Sitting in the space between Ray and Lenny was a haggard, thinning man with torn clothing and unkempt facial hair. His presence felt like a sloppy edit of a bad movie, like he was in the wrong scene and made to pretend that he was actually there before Ray. The boy looked at him, but it didn't feel like the figure was really *there* at all as he still sat in a pile of rubble in some dirt cellar that couldn't be perceived by sight alone. He somehow existed in two spaces at once. Despite that, the impossible man clearly did see him, and Ray looked upon Yarbrough like a zombie that had forced his damned soul out of hell itself. But it was the fact that Yarbrough no longer had legs that caused Ray to wretch.

Sickness rose in Ray's gut as he tried to take this sight in, but he couldn't quite process any of it. The half-dead man sitting in the space in reality between the two cousins smiled up at the boy and wiped the dried blood staining his teeth and crusted lips.

"You look like you've seen a ghost."

As the shadows broke their way into the underwater city far below them, Ray could only think of all the people trapped in their slowly dying paradise. Where would they go when the wave of darkness swallowed them whole?

Soon enough, ghosts would be all that remained of Lenny's new world. This time, there would be no second chance at life. This was truly the end of it all.

Part Four
Baptism into Death

The madness of the situation unscrambled as Ray faced the source of his troubles. His favorite cousin and his former enemy each lay before him, just as they did a year ago, but now they appeared to be on opposite sides and not altogether whole anymore. The shadows continued to grow below them as they faced each other down.

Just by looking at the former leader of the Panorama Agents, Ray could tell that something was very different. His face was even paler than it was the last time he'd seen him, sheet white like a ghost. He also smelled of congealed blood and sewage, his skin slashed up and bruised, and this was before bringing up his missing legs. Ray did not see this many wounds on him when the boy first arrived here. Where exactly had he been over the past year? Yarbrough existed between spaces, his form immaterial like a mirage in the desert.

"You brought me here," Ray said. "You caused this."

The haggard guitar player coughed, hacking up what looked like red phlegm. After a brief fit, he finally replied. "Who else could I call that might resist what they see here? I thought you and your little friend would be a bit more skeptical. You did, after all, both see the Y Signal before, and you both understand the world isn't as simple as Mommy and Daddy say it is. Looks like my hopes were too high. Your friend is in the thick of it as much as anyone else."

"Shut your mouth!" Ray found himself yelling for reasons he couldn't even comprehend. "You don't know what we've been through since you screwed everything up a year ago. Nothing is what it used to be because of you."

"So it's only been a year for you, huh? After you stopped the Y Signal, I fell between the sheets. Those apes chased me down and hunted me for ages through that dark jungle, and I barely escaped with my life. Finally, I found my way here—the Paradise I thought I had sought. And yet, when I arrived, I quickly realized it was a false Eden. No one wanted to hear it; they didn't believe in the apes hiding in the dark. They cast me out for telling the truth, all so they could continue living their lie. Isn't that right, Lenny? Now there is nothing left of me except the remains you see before you."

Lenny glanced away for a moment. "They couldn't be happy with you there."

"Better uncomfortable than dead," Yarbrough said. He coughed violently, reeling back in his sitting position. He finally flopped over onto his back in the rubble. "Your dumb cousin is here, Lenny. Time to wrap it up."

"Wrap *what* up?" Ray asked. He looked between the pair, but no answer arrived from either of them. "If this isn't that Paradise you were looking for, then what is it?"

"Something to the left of Agartha." Yarbrough closed his eyes and grit his teeth. "Just off enough to make all the difference."

"Another world? Country? Planet? What?"

"The same functional difference. The only difference is that this one was always a cheap copy, and now its wearing out."

Whatever that meant was far beyond Ray's capability for understanding. These two were clearly deeper in something a stupid kid wouldn't even begin to comprehend. Instead, he looked back to his cousin again. "If it's not Paradise or whatever, then leave. Come home, Lenny. We've been waiting for a year."

Lenny brought his attention back to the town underneath the water again. The edges warbled with the swimming shadows beating at the boundaries. "It's taking all my concentration to keep the city submerged under the waves and protected from outside forces. Once the barrier gives, the physical world we built will meet this outer space, and it will all be lost in the torrent. Don't ask me how I know it: I can just tell. This town is like a part of me now. When it dies, I'll feel it inside. I don't know where we'll end up, Ray. I don't even know where *you* will end up. I can't just turn it off like it's a stereo system I'm bored with. Other people are at stake."

"It was a pure shadow play. Kids playing house." Yarbrough coughed hard again. His body wracked as he rocked in place in the rubble. The former rocker flattened himself out on the dirt, staring up at the endless blue sky above him. When he finally quieted up, Ray broke the silence.

"I was an idiot to think this place was real. Every bit of it was an illusion, Lenny? You made it for them? Does anyone down there even know what you've done? You think you're some kind of god that can mess with people's heads, all so you can live in a fantasy world. Even without those shadows, this is messed up."

Lenny grimaced. "Arriving here first allowed me the chance to build a space for us all, but I did it with the assumption that we had reached Paradise—that it would allow us to stay. I didn't want to believe Yarbrough's words. It's fading fast now."

"Make up your minds," Yarbrough said. "Do you stay and live out your last moments in a fake dream, or do you gamble leaving it behind? I know what I'd choose." He paused and then laughed through his coughs as if he had just heard a funny joke. He soon fell quiet.

Ray glimpsed the wide open sky, thin lines of shadow highlighting the cracks he couldn't quite see. Every piece of this place was artificial. "What did you choose, Yarbrough?"

But the rock star didn't answer. Ray turned back to find Yarbrough had completely vanished as if he were never even there to begin with. Ray, in fact, never heard his voice again.

The world blacked like bad fluorescent lights flickering in a dark hallway. Ray tried to rub his eyes but couldn't feel either his eyes or his arms. The boy had been left in the abyss.

And then he wasn't anymore.

The light returned, and Ray found himself in his cousin's old apartment, the piercing light of the sunrise blocking the view out the window where the balcony lay. Beside him, Lenny sat on the couch. He now looked exactly like Ray remembered him being, the same disheveled young man who disappeared after that visit to Sophie's Pizzeria a year ago. Lenny smiled weakly at his cousin and patted the cushion next to him. Ray joined him, and the two stared at the television.

On the screen was an old action game starring military jeeps that he could not remember the name of. It had been years since Ray last played this one. Lenny handed his cousin a controller, and the two began playing this old game.

"It isn't that hard," Lenny said. "We can beat it."

"I'm mostly used to the 16-bit systems these days. It's going to take time to adjust."

"Most people move on to the newest thing when they can. Can't blame them. Who wants to be left behind? But sometimes it's more fun to pick up a classic."

"I guess." Ray took his jeep across the beach level, throwing grenades and rescuing POWs in enemy bases. He had little problem at all readjusting to it all. Lenny was right, this one was a classic. "Maybe I'll hook up my NES back up when I get home. Mom was pestering me to sell it."

"Old things have to make way for new things."

"It's just a game. Fun is fun. Don't see what age has to do with it. According to the magazines, they're pushing for 3D over these sorts of games. Not sure how I feel about that. Games won't play the same."

"You either adjust or get left out, Ray. That's how it works." Lenny fired a rocket at the final tank boss on level one. It exploded and the victory fanfare played. "All those people have nowhere to go, and I'm not sure I can bring them back home with me. Some of them have never known anything but this place."

"But it's all a lie."

"So what?"

That familiar jingle for level two started, and Ray found himself humming it without even thinking. He had almost forgotten he wasn't back home, and things weren't as they used to be. "You can't stay here, Lenny. You don't have a choice."

"I know this place isn't Paradise. There is no immortality, time passes, even if no one really knows how it does, and people do die. We just don't talk about it. I don't know how long ago we arrived; no one does. But what happens when I use what little influence I have to throw us out of here? Where will we end up? It might be somewhere worse."

"You have to try. You brought people like Billy here. You owe him."

"He works at a rental store, of all things, and he loves it. Never would have expected it from him. He doesn't even need pills to sleep anymore."

"If you can do that for him, you can also do something better, Lenny. I trust you. I always have."

The two continued playing, Ray relishing destroying the living statues attempting to make their lives a problem. He couldn't help expressing his surprise that he still remembered how to play this one as well as he had. Finally, after beating the second stage boss, he turned to his cousin.

"Yarbrough thought he had it all figured out, remember. Then I screwed it up for him. The guy who thought he knew the future didn't see me coming. Last winter, too, a bunch of us ended up nearly dying thanks to one of your old friends. Who knows what will happen tomorrow?"

"Brad was always too unstable. We never should have trusted the Y Signal. We just thought it knew the future. It got so much right."

"Some of the things it talked about a year ago didn't happen."

"Some did."

"Yeah, *some*," Ray said. "A lot of it, from what I remembered, was guessing, right? What that tells me is that it didn't really know the future. The Y Signal was either guessing as best it could, or it knew some things and bluffed the rest. Maybe, it was even lying about some things on purpose. I don't know its game. No one will now. But, you were taking it as gospel truth, when we know it's not."

"Did your dad ever ask about me?"

The boy went back to the game. Stage three was a lot tougher than the first two, but still Ray somehow remembered it well. He had only died once, and it kept him on his toes as his machine gun mowed into the enemy jeeps. They might actually beat this whole thing in one sitting.

"*I* want you back, Lenny," Ray said. "Why isn't that enough? It's already bad enough without Granny. Most of my friends are already gone, and I start at a terrible school in a few months. Things aren't exactly looking up right now. Having you come back would be enough."

"What if leaving this behind kills us all?"

"This place is dying." Ray paused the game and looked at his cousin dead in the eyes. "What choice do you have? It's a chance, or it's certain death. I know what I want. What about you?"

Lenny stared back at his cousin for a moment. Finally, he stood up and approached the blinding windows where the bright sun shone in. Outside was that balcony Ray knew too well. Lenny tapped his fingers on the window-sill. "It's been so long. What if this was all for nothing?"

"It wasn't."

"How do you know, Ray? Staying here was the only time I felt like what I did mattered at all. I don't want to go back to being dust in the wind."

"You never were, man. This whole thing started because someone took a guess at a bigger plan and tried to change *their place* in it, right? It's all about what you choose to do, isn't it? You can be anything, and you can go anywhere! Even if you don't end up back home with me, maybe you'll go somewhere else, wherever your path takes you and find something better. But that will never happen if you let it all end here in that deathtrap. Granny wouldn't have wanted that—I don't want that."

"All of the others left home for a reason, and those born here know nothing else." He turned back to face Ray again. "What if they end up like I was—or like Yarbrough?"

"You're going to have to trust someone eventually, right? Why not me? Have I ever steered you wrong? I might still be a kid, but I don't lie. Just like you."

Ray's cousin sighed. He glanced around the apartment, the old furniture and pictures on the wall were the way they were before he disappeared. The place no longer looked like this back home, where his grandmother took it over before his father sold it after her death, but that hardly mattered. Somewhere, someplace, it still looked as it always did and always would. Lenny nodded to himself and bit his lip as if in thought. He sat down on the couch beside his cousin again, grabbing the controller.

"We'll beat these punks," Lenny said. "We can do it."

Ray smiled and unpaused the game. The mood shifted to something reminiscent of the old days where they joked amongst each other and debated calling for a pizza they could not even send for. It was nice, even if fleeting. Lenny was finally acting like the person Ray knew so well, his laughter as honest as it once was long ago. It was at that moment that he also remembered his cousin's strange words from long ago in Sophie's Pizzeria.

"*Life is a dream, desperate to be swept away. Dew-covered grass in the morning is always withered by night. But we ain't grass!*"

He had an inkling of what that meant now, even if his cousin hadn't understood it himself at the time.

The pair beat the game, and Ray knew it was time to go home. There were people waiting for him.

There always would be someone, somewhere.

Part Five
Fade Away

The humid basement hit him like a bullet train, dragging Ray's energy down almost instantly upon entry. The summer weather felt like he had experienced it for the first time. In a way, he had, though it had also been ages since the last time he'd seen this place. At least, that's what he thought. How long had he actually been gone for?

The headache rushed in and blurred his vision. The boy stumbled into a stack of chairs, knocking them to the floor, the resulting echo reverberated through the basement. The light tapping of water rocked from somewhere above. Was it raining? He slowly trod towards the stairs, glad to put this all behind him.

"What did you do, Ray?" Andrew asked.

Ray spotted Andrew sitting on the stairs back out of the basement. He was wearing his slightly unkempt suit from graduation, just like Ray was, only now he sat there scratching his scalp as if it were crawling with bugs. The two of them really were back home again. His taller friend didn't look happy about it.

"Sorry, Andrew," Ray said. "I had to do it."

"Why?"

"It wasn't real."

"George is gone, Danny's turned weird, and now I have to leave." He stood up, rage contorted on his sweating face. "You didn't even get Lenny back, man. What was the point of all that?"

"Andrew, that place was falling apart. It was either come back, or lose ourselves in that void, you know, like what happened to Yarbrough. We could have even died. Is that what you wanted? You saw those ape-men—you even fought one before! You know what was out there trying to get at us. We had to come back home. Did you think you could stay there forever?"

Ray's friend ran down the stairs and seized the shorter boy's lapels. "Yeah, it's what I wanted. I wanted a place where I can stay, where everything is the way it was supposed to be. What's wrong with that? Why do I have to lose what I want? Who do you think you are taking that from me?"

"Well, too bad." Ray shoved Andrew back. "It was dying, Andrew. Lenny had been there for so long and even he didn't fully get it until we talked it out. The choice was between death or a chance at life. He made his decision. We're better off back home."

"Home for some of us."

"What does that mean?" Ray asked.

Andrew's fist trembled under his friend's nose for a second too long before he grunted and punched the wall. Chips of concrete littered the boy's knuckles. "Lenny's gone, yeah, but so is George. Danny's parents are talking about sending him to military school. That's what we were arguing about upstairs. He doesn't care about anything these days. His grandfather had a stroke, and now his family is fighting over his freaking house. He doesn't trust anyone anymore. And then there's me. I won't be here for seventh grade. I don't get to have my life either. There's nothing here for me."

"I'm sorry about your parents, Andrew, but that place wasn't going to fix them. You know it wouldn't."

"I know!" Andrew yelled.

"Then what do you want? I can't change this, man."

"It's just—"

"What? Spell it out for me. What do you think I or anyone else can do about the way things are? Thing's change; people change. It's not just stupid movie stuff. You don't think I want Lenny back? My grandmother? George? But they're gone, and all for very different reasons. Sometimes, I guess we don't get what we want. You can't live like Yarbrough, man. We know where that kind of thing leads."

The taller boy turned on his heel and stared up the stairs towards the door. Light from the hallways shone through the cracks, but it remained dull, possibly due to the rain. There was a long pause before Andrew spoke again.

"It was supposed to be simple, Ray. We make it through this school crap; we move out and get normal jobs, get married to babes and have some kids, and then we all get together at school reunions and talk about it. Simple. That's what my folks said it would be before they decided to give up."

"Give up? Weren't they in counseling for awhile? That's trying, isn't it?"

"They gave up." Andrew turned back towards Ray again. "Even if I wasn't leaving, we both know things aren't the same. They were changing before any of this happened. You know, it hasn't always been great, but we did have the guys, our 'rents, and people and places we saw every day. It all reminded me that you can always make it to summer vacation if you're tough enough. There's always another summer. But that's gone now, right? I've got my dog, and that's it."

"Barney is a good dog, but he's not *it*. We're still friends. You're thinking too hard, Andrew. It's been a weird year, yeah, but it's only been one year. Remember when I first heard the Y Signal, and I thought I was hearing the future? Not all of that stuff came true."

"Some of it did."

"You sound like Lenny. Are you going to stress out over maybes? That's not you."

Andrew furrowed his brow. "How can you just ignore everything that happened? How can you pretend that it wasn't the greatest time of your life? How can you not want to go back?"

It took all Ray had to smile at his perturbed friend. He put his hands in his pockets were his fists involuntarily balled up."I promised Lenny. I have to make up for what he couldn't do."

"And what's that?"

"To show that we can live here. We don't have to run, like he did. If our parents can make it work, then so can we. The world's been around forever, and it'll be around much longer than we will. Nothing ever stays the same. You know that, I know that. Why did we think the world would stop with us?"

Andrew pursed his lip as if in question but never replied. Instead, he shook his head, and marched up the stairs. Ray followed him out of the basement.

The restaurant was still rather empty aside from the large party room. The two boys rejoined the group as if nothing was wrong, merging into the crowd. Even the rain Ray thought he had heard appeared to have vanished, leaving only the beaming sun shining through the large windows across the carpeting and old hardwood. Andrew sat with a group of girls, chatting and smiling as if nothing had happened. Ray watched him from his old seat in the corner.

Andrew never looked back over. It appeared that their conversation had ended, and he was moving on from it.

"How did it work out?" Kristin asked. She sat beside him again, a wrinkle of worry on her brow. "Danny stormed out of here a few minutes ago. Was there a fight? Did you get square with Andrew again?"

Somehow, it only having been a short time since Ray went to the basement didn't surprise him that much. He would never truly know how long he was gone for. "No, but the issue is settled. We're good. But enough about them. Say, do you play video games?"

"Who doesn't? I've got a Super NES at home, and I'm really good at *Super Mario World*. My dad plays it sometimes, too. Why do you ask?"

He took a glance at Andrew who never once stopped his conversation with the girls. A calmness washed over Ray at the realization that this was how it should be. Sixth grade was done.

"Feel like coming over sometime?" he asked Kristin. "I've got some classics I need to dig out, and I don't think the guys are interested."

She pursed her lips in thought before smiling back at him. "Sure, what do you got?"

"Well, there is this game on the old NES, right? In this one you play as these jeeps . . ."

The party went on into the evening, excitement at an all time high. Friends shared stories, teachers said their farewells, teachers got oddly sappy, and the dinner was surprisingly tasty. Ray didn't regret attending, though he did wish he had has parents there like most everyone else did.

The graduation party would eventually fall into obscurity, no one thinking about it much again for the rest of their lives. It would just become a vague thought hiding in the depths of their memories. Even Ray would go on to forget their faces and names, but they would still remained buried deep down. Children are resilient, but they do remember more than most believe they can. These days would always stick to them as an expectation, a hope, for it to be matched in the years ahead. No one would say so out loud, or probably even realize it themselves, but it remained a truth. What came down the road would always be tainted with expectation based on what had already happened.

As time went on, all would go their separate ways, and almost none would meet again outside of memory, dreams, and reunions made specifically to reassess those happy days. Somewhere inside would always remain the hope that such a feeling could be revisited again, but life does not allow two joys to be quite the same. This day would fade away, but nothing could erase that it happened, and that what occurred would ripple on into the future in ways the attendees couldn't possibly understand. Time rolls as it rolls.

After Ray was picked up by his family, when the dinner was over, and the sun fell from the sky, he knew, on some level, that all of this was true, even if he didn't have a way of expressing it at his younger age. The boy understood he would never see Andrew or his other friends again, and he was right to think so; but at that moment, it felt almost like a dream—like it wasn't real. Someday, he would wake up to the real world.

But what was real? This was more than what he could see, hear, or touch. The Y Signal showed that there was more that he would never experience, at least in this world. So what could he do but keep searching for the real deal? What lay out in the world, hidden by the mundane repetition of everyday life and expectation of the banal? There had to be more, even beyond that long-dead signal. He would spend the rest of his days seeking it out.

Maybe that was how it was always meant to be.

"Did you have a good time, Ray?" his mother asked.

The lampposts flickered on as if guiding the car onward into the burgeoning night. The radio played one of those "ska" songs he had heard about from the guys at school, bouncing in a happy rhythm as horns played their chirpy blasts. Meanwhile, his father swore at a minivan that cut him off, and Ray's brother slept soundly in the seat beside him as his mother placed a blanket over the little guy. Despite how typical it all was, Ray couldn't fight off the gratitude he felt for all this nonsense he had gotten so used to in the short years he spent on this world.

That was a feeling he would never lose, no matter what madness awaited him in the years to come.

"Yeah, I did."

Part Six
Many Futures

The summer heat was getting brutal these days, but it wasn't going to bring down his mood. He had been through too much. The preteen stepped into Sophie's Pizzeria, grateful that he was at least out of the sun. The familiar 1950s décor and pictures on the wall were an odd source of comfort to him when he sat down at one of the tables. It reminded him of warm moments and happy times, even if it was where one of his darkest memories began. The place was oddly empty today, though that might have been due to the early afternoon hour. Adults were still at work, and most kids and teenagers were at the arcade or the park.

The two visitors made their order in the pleasant silence of the restaurant. It was far more comfortable than he expected it to be.

Ray's father sat across from the preteen, grunting as the chair shifted under him. "This is why I prefer eating at home."

"You never want to go out, Dad."

"Comes with being tired after work. One week off isn't going to give me energy like you kids. So, why did you want to come here so much?"

The place had looked the same ever since Ray was a kid, but there was always a strange comfort in coming here. Choosing when and where to go out gave him a sense of control. It might have been silly, but he would take whatever he could get these days. This summer had been wild enough. "How long has Sophie's been around?"

His father waved to a middle-aged waitress talking behind the counter to the teenage cashier. "Started when I was a kid in the '60s. Sophie herself opened this place up with her sister-in-law, and the kids used to always come by here on the weekends. It was always full." Ray's father pointed at the old pictures on the walls. "She sure loved celebrity pictures. Strange that no matter how much time passes, this place doesn't change. These days, I think the kids hang out in the mall or the arcade instead, right? That's where you always go. Sophie's today is mostly for dads who pick it up on the way home from work for their kids. Then again, Pizza Hut is getting more and more popular . . ."

"It was a year ago when I met Lenny here," Ray said. He didn't even know why he felt the need to say it, but the words came easy. "He disappeared right after we met."

Ray's father sighed and rubbed his temples. "You're going to bring this up again?"

"Do you ever think about him, Dad? He said he didn't have the best relationship with his own father. But he liked you. He always wanted to know what you thought of him."

"He wouldn't have liked his dad since that dirtbag left his family a long time ago. Lenny only really had his mother. Shame about the accident. You never met her, did you, Ray? Strong woman, always there when you needed her. It was always a good time when she was around. Anyway, how about we try mini-putt after this? It's been a long time since we've done that. I know Keith and his kids go there a lot. I'll take you on and whup you good, shrimp."

"Are you really not worried about Lenny at all? Shouldn't somebody be?"

His father looked into his son's eyes with an inscrutable expression. "Ray, what do you think worrying about him is going to do? He isn't here anymore. Your grandmother, much as I miss her, went to the police, and they couldn't find anything. No evidence, no sightings, no motivation for anything involving foul play. Those thugs they found outside his place were interrogated many times, and none of them had the means or motivation to either hurt him or hide anything they did. It was a miracle they got to Burroughsvale in the first place, considering how much of a mess their lives were. Lenny's out there somewhere. As of this point, it's up to him to come back. I wouldn't turn him away if he decided to knock on my door. But worrying about that isn't going to do anything. What's wrong with you today, anyway? Are you still having those dreams?"

"No, not since graduation." It was true that Ray hadn't seen anything since the last time he had met Lenny in that strange dream world, and the Y Signal was nothing but a memory now; yet he couldn't help but wonder. As it faded further into memory, he started doubting how much of it was actually real. "Dad, do you ever think about tomorrow, like a long time from now?"

"You mean the future?" Ray's dad sat back in his chair. He curled a lip as if he wanted a cigarette, but he had left his pack in the car. Instead, he sighed. "What is to worry about, Ray? You live in the greatest period in history. Sure, it's not the '60s, but it's the next best thing. You have a safe neighborhood, you're about to enter a decent school. You've also got a family, friends, and a good job market for when you graduate. All you have to do is put in the work, and you will get everything you'll ever need. Why worry?"

Traces of those visions clung to the back of Ray's mind. That world where youth merged with immortality in the illusions resembled something close to what he remembered as the best parts of his childhood, mixed with his deeply embedded expectations for the future. Could anything really live up to that place? He had been taught that going through the motions was how one got through life, but the past year had challenged all those perceptions. As the Y Signal's predictions turned out to be both correct and incorrect in equal turns, and as his mind slowly purged that trauma from his memories, all he had been left with was the realization that he was a clueless preteen in over his head. Civilization was about safety. Wasn't it?

"Do you believe in fate, Dad?"

His father blinked. "Where did that come from?"

"But do you?"

"Mystical crap is a waste of time."

"How?"

"I don't think about it. No time. Work's enough of a pain, and then I come home and have to make sure the rest of you have a roof over your head and food on your plates. That's what's important. Just do what you have to. What else can you do?"

"I can't stop thinking about Granny and Lenny, or the guys. They all did what they were supposed to, and now they're all gone. Did they make the wrong choices, or was that their destiny?"

"You will eventually accept it," Ray's father said. "That's just life. People come and go for no reason, and sometimes they die. You get used to it. Beating your fists against concrete is a good way to break your hands. Now here comes the waitress. She finally stopped lecturing that girl at the register. Eat up quickly. By the way, how does it feel to be a graduate? That doesn't happen every day."

"I don't feel any different."

"You will."

"Do I have to?"

"That's life, Ray. You can't stop it."

The pizza was the same as it always was, but it tasted a bit different, stronger. Perhaps there was too much sauce, but it left a bitter tinge on his tongue as it mixed with the soft, doughy crust. That was Ray's last summer of his childhood, in a nutshell. He would meet new friends and go to a new school soon enough, and eventually, these events would fade into memory until most of it was a misty haze of childhood wistfulness. The Y Signal never darkened his door again, and his worried and seemingly real dreams also slowly faded away.

As his father drove them towards the mini-putt range, Ray caught a glance of his old school—the one he would never step foot in again. He remembered those tall fences and the cracked building of that distant world. Lenny was still out there, somewhere, in this huge universe, but Ray knew deep down that he would never see him again. All of this would be left behind in the rear-view, just like Sophie's Pizzeria was at that very moment.

But what else was out there? His father didn't seem to care, but Ray couldn't help but think about what he would never know. As they drove through the familiar streets of Burroughsvale that Ray had been a part of forever, he now saw them a bit differently. How many streets were out there beyond his hometown that he would never have the chance to go down? How many roundabouts and dead-ends could there possibly be in the thousands of cities, villages, and towns, in the world? He would never know, and somehow, that prospect was more exciting to him than what remained of his last real summer.

They passed the field that the guys once played so many games in. Ray remembered the war that he and Andrew won by the skin of their teeth, celebrating at Kevin's birthday party the next day with plenty of cake and two-player Sega Genesis games. It was also the place where they got into a fight with Adam and Aaron's friends in a brawl for the ages. Once they won, he got chewed out by his mom and secretly given a pat on the back from his dad. It got wild in Burroughsvale when the boys cut loose.

The convenience store owned by the Conte family still stood on the corner where it always did. Kristin's sister quit working there not long after Christmas, and they had a hard time finding a replacement. That was also where Ray and his friends got sick on sweets and promised never to do anything stupid again. He laughed as he thought on how much of a failure that plan had turned out to be.

The hot sun shone, and the crisp wind blew through the rolled down car windows. On the radio, "Follow You Down" by the Gin Blossoms gave way to "1979" by the Smashing Pumpkins. It all made sense, in that moment. The sights, the sounds, the feel, and even the taste, merged into one experience he could only define as "summer vacation" to anyone who would ask. Even as the years melted away and the cast of characters in his life shrank, grew, and changed, Ray would never forget the feeling of this one moment that would be otherwise lost to time, like so many others that he once thought so important.

For that one second, everything was right with the world, and nothing else mattered but the road itself.

But he knew that everything did matter. Every choice, every word, and every action made, had led him to that exact moment, and it was almost all worth it just for that single second of an epiphany in an otherwise normal day. Even as the years went by and tragedies, joys, and yet more strangeness, passed over his life, in the depths of his being he would never forget that one water-drop in the ocean of his life. Even now where the madness and the insanity of the Y Signal was but a memory, his bones would always know the truth. Who was to say he would never feel that way again?

Who knew anything that was to come in the roller-coaster ahead? In that second, he was content not knowing anything except that he knew nothing.

Today was just another day, and that was more than enough for the preteen. A laugh burst from his stomach, confusing his own father who questioned if he was actually okay. He was, and that simple sensation was enough for him.

Ray hoped he would never lose that feeling again.

WHY NOW

The setting sun falls over you as you fire the last shots from your rifle. You roll down the hill, your friends laughing and yelling at each other as the bullets cut them all down. The game went on all afternoon, but no one protested. It wasn't until now, as you all lay on that steep slope, hard breaths pumping, that it all made sense. The deep orange light tinting the sky in your old neighborhood brought a sense of familiar comfort over you. Jokes were passed around about who died first and who narrowly avoided losing their lives. The night was fast coming on, but still you all chatted like you had plenty of time left.

One by one, your friends got up and left, waving as they abandoned their prone positions on the battlefield to return home. There would always be a next time.

Eventually, you were left alone and stood up at the top of the old hill. The oncoming night told you it was time to go home, even if the cold never arrived to nudge you onward. You marched down the slope to see one of your friends waiting for you, looking the same as you remembered him from long ago. He would always look like that in your mind's eye, no matter how much time passed or life beat him down. Here, you were both as you once were in the past, and nothing else mattered but this moment.

"Sorry, I never came back," he says to you.

You shrug. "I never expected you to. Things were crazy for all of us back then, and it never really stopped. How did it work out for you?"

"Not so good, at first. Both sides of my family got into this big fight after my aunt died. It was about money this, and inheritance that. You probably went through something like it; everyone eventually does. I spent most of high school in and out of detention halls or worse. It turned it around, somehow. I managed to find myself a good girl, and we had a couple of kids far away from the place I was born. We moved around a lot, looking for home. Pretty typical stuff. How about you?"

You remembered the last time you saw your old best friend.

It was back in the summer when you graduated from elementary school, sixth grade, and after you had just seen your world turned upside down by forces outside your control. He was there with you for that moment, but despite your former closeness, you had never reconnected after he left. The world just kept going, leaving it all behind in the haze. The two of you had lost contact, and life never let you fix that. At least, that was your excuse.

"Kristin and I found her sister after we graduated high school," you say. "She had joined some weird compound cult. It took some talking, but we got her and her new family out of there. Kristin and I tied the knot, but we also never came back home. By the time we left, there was nothing left of the place we grew up in. It became something different for different people."

"Did you ever find Lenny?"

You shake your head in the negative. "That's what I'm doing now."

"I'm sure he's here if all the guys are. This is the reunion we were always too scared or stupid to create for ourselves."

"We could have done it anytime."

"But we didn't," he says. "Nothing ever stopped us from doing this. Might have been different if someone would have picked up a phone. Guess we'll never know now."

There is no way the pause that follows your brief exchange doesn't contain an awkwardness you both desperately want to extinguish, but there is little you can do but let it be. You long learned to accept the way things are. You just let it melt away with the setting sun. It is more important that you finally saw your friend again and that things, as different as they might be, somehow remained the same despite the times changing you both.

You would always be those dumb kids at heart.

"It was nice seeing the boys again," you say.

He smiles. "I missed the old neighborhood. By the time I remembered to look it up online, it was all gone already, unrecognizable. Unfamiliar names, torn down or repaved buildings and streets, and all the faces were of strangers. Felt almost like I was erased, like I was never there at all. Gave me some perspective on it all. Got to thinking if any of those good and bad times ever happened to begin with, or if I imagined it. Your mind can play tricks on you without evidence to cling to or remind you. Since I'm here with you, I guess it was real after all. Load off my mind."

"Where are you going now?"

"I've got to talk to a few people. I'm sure you do, too. Also, I should say I'm sorry I never got in touch again. I think I'll always regret that."

"I was just like you," you say. "We also left town, never looked back. Kristin and I roamed the country, had some kids, and tried to settle down, but I always thought of Burroughsvale, and those moments with the guys and my family in our hometown. No place ever felt like it did, no matter where we went. We were always alone together."

"That's just the way it is. Life never takes you were you expect. Anyways, I'll catch you later."

He turns on his heel, and begins walking down the street. You call after him, but your friend only waves as he slowly disappears down those familiar sidewalks long since gone from the neighborhood of your youth. He says one thing to you over his shoulder before he is gone again.

"*Life is a dream, desperate to be swept away. Dew-covered grass in the morning is always withered by night. But we ain't grass!*"

You remember those words from long ago. You remember a lot of things now. The more you walk these long forgotten streets of your abandoned youth, the vacant roads and lawns, the sidewalks lost to time, the more prominent they become in your mind. In the windows of the nearby apartments, you think you see familiar faces that shuffle about as they always did on summer evenings in the old neighborhood, the rest after a long day of work. This old town is alive, but with a very different feeling from the way you remember it back then.

The more you journey forward, the more the silence mixes in with the chatter of departed voices and sounds of a place long since left to the fog of time. It all swirls together like cream in coffee, until it is all but one uniform parade of existence in your mind where every piece slides in together in marching unison. It becomes more coherent the more you see the old sights, the old people, the old sky, and the old world that had once passed away. Here it has all returned, as if it never left in the first place and, in some ways, it never really had. All of that uncertainty and doubt rolls off you like rain off rubber. You know where you are going now.

Up ahead, the sunset has already given way to the night, but the dark is masked itself by a strange starlight much brighter than the one you are used to. It is as if the sky itself has lit lampposts for you to walk under, but the light is everywhere in this, your old neighborhood. The wind blows cool air against the back of your neck, but no cold enters you.

At the edge of the road, you spot your cousin, waiting by a bus stop on the corner. He isn't as you remember seeing him last. His eyes are less-clouded, younger, his clothes clean and his hair combed. He smiles wide at your arrival. You stop, your mouth ajar as you look him over. The last time you saw him was a lifetime ago in a far different place than this. He laughs as you notice the pair of bikes at his side, waving you towards one of them. Somehow, you are able to accept that it is not only him, but that he is not the last person you will see on this journey into this open unknown. You now understand the next adventure awaiting ahead for everyone in this place.

"Been a while, huh?" he asks you. "We've got a lot to see."

You grab your bike and sit beside him. "Where are we going?"

"Anywhere and everywhere. Just wait until you see what I found up ahead. You won't believe it!"

ABOUT THE AUTHOR

JD Cowan is a writer with an obsession for stories and Truth. He takes pleasure in looking for Light in the places where darkness grips the tightest. His works include Grey Cat Blues, The Pulp Mindset, Someone is Aiming for You & Other Adventures, The Last Fanatics, and stories in Cirsova, Storyhack, the PulpRev Sampler, and the Planetary Anthology Series. His works can found at Amazon.

He blogs at wastelandandsky.blogspot.ca and can be found on Twitter @wastelandJD for those interested.

WORKS

Books

Brutal Dreams
Someone is Aiming for You & Other Adventures
Grey Cat Blues
Knights of the End
Y Signal
Gemini Man Trilogy

Non-Fiction

The Pulp Mindset: A NewPub Survival Guide
Generation Y: The New Lost Generation *[with Brian Niemeier and David V. Stewart]*
The Last Fanatics

Anthologies

The PulpRev Sampler
Corona-Chan: Spreading the Love
Pulp Rock
Sidearm & Sorcery, Vol. 1
Pulp On Pulp: Tips & Tricks for Writing Pulp Fiction
Planetary Uranus
Planetary Sol